THE LION

CLAN ROSS OF THE HEBRIDES

Pink Door Publishing

Editor: Dark Dreams Editing

© Hildie McQueen 2021
Print Edition

ISBN: 978-1-939356-90-1

Also By Hildie McQueen

ABOUT THE BOOK

Preferring to spend time outdoors sketching and not worrying overmuch about her appearance, Isobel Macdonald is shocked when a handsome laird chooses her to marry. However, as one who treasures loyalty above all, she is mortified to learn his lover lives at the family keep as well. After being publicly humiliated by her new husband, Isobel must ensure two things: to keep her heart protected, and to remain a wife in name only.

After his late father's time as laird, where he ruled by fear, Darach Ross inherits a clan of people who do not trust in him, or his leadership. With the threat of insurrection and possible attack by another clan, every move he makes must be measured. When he is captured by an enemy clan and forced to face the possibility of leaving no legacy, he makes a mistake that could rob him of happiness forever.

Laird Calum Ross was dead. His eldest son, thirty-four-year-old, Darach Finlay Ross has inherited the lairdship and control over the vast lands on the Isle of Uist.

In the months that follow, Darach learns of the atrocities his father committed against the clan and must work hard to regain their trust. However, when he discovers that someone within the clan is plotting against him, he is faced with his biggest challenge yet: An execution.

Each of the seven Ross siblings must come to terms with

their new roles as leaders responsible for hundreds of families.

One by one, they will find their calling, their place, and hopefully a love for all time.

A FEW NOTES

Dear Reader,

This fictional story takes place at the beginning of the 17th century in the Scottish Hebrides, isles off the Isle of Skye's western coast.

In the 1500s, lordship over the Hebrides collapsed and the power was given to clan chiefs. The MacNeil in Barra. The Macdonald (Clanranald) in South Uist. The Uisdein in North Uist. The MacLeod the isles of Harris and Lewis.

For this series, I have moved the clans around a bit to help the story work better. The clans' locations in my books are as follows. The MacNeil will remain in Barra. The Macdonald (Clanranald) is moved to North Uist. The Uisdein resides in Benbecula. The MacLeod remains in the Isles of Harris and Lewis. My fictional clan, Clan Ross, will be laird over South Uist.

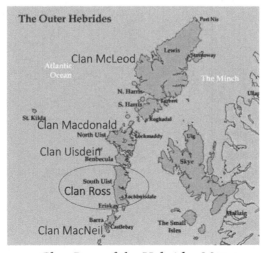

Clan Ross of the Hebrides Map

CHAPTER ONE

Dún Láidir, Keep Ross
Summer 1601

T HE LOUD ARGUMENT between the men that stood before
him did not deter others in the great hall from trying to
be heard above their shouts. Another group of people stood in
a circle to the side yelling insults. Behind the group, a pair of
men were tied at the wrists with guards standing watch, as the
binds did not keep them from kicking at each other.

A fire had been lit in the hearth that morning, while it was
still cold in the room and now the combination of the heat and
stench of unwashed bodies crammed into the space made it
overwhelmingly difficult to concentrate.

Darach Ross, pushed back a lock of blond hair that fell
over his brow and leaned forward in an attempt to hear what
the supplicants before him were arguing about, but he was
barely able to decipher their issues since both yelled at each
other more than trying to explain their complaints to him.

When he could not get the men to settle, he looked to his
brother Stuart who was leaning forward staring at the men as
if attempting to read their lips. His brother's hazel gaze moved
from one man to the other, while he fiddled with an arrow in
his hands.

"I cannot hear what is being said. Is it possible to remove

some of the people to another space?" Darach asked Cairn McKinney, a member of his council, who sat to his right.

The older man looked from one side of the room to the other, and Darach did the same, taking in the desperate expressions of those present. Every person in the room was looking to him to somehow fix their situation. Most were dirty and much too thin, with the pale hollow eyes of someone with no hope.

Hunger he could help with; disillusionment and distrust were another story.

Upon realizing Darach was distracted, the men in front of him became furious and began screaming at him directly.

"Do ye even hear me, Laird?" one yelled.

"Ye do not care, do ye?" the other screamed.

"Enough!" Darach roared and stood to his full height, towering over the men from the high board. "I am yer laird and will not tolerate insolence."

At Darach's exclamation, the room quieted. The silence was short-lived because just then on the far side of the crowded room a fight broke out. The pair who'd been bound had somehow gotten loose and were now brawling. When they fell onto a table, the people there just cheered and shoved them away.

The guardsmen in the room pushed their way through the crowd to the fighters, pulled the men apart, and dragged them out to the courtyard. People jeered loudly at the end of their entertainment.

Darach motioned for one of his personal guards to come closer.

"I want twenty warriors to come at once. Enough of this

unruliness. Take those in the back half of the room outside. Except for the women and children. They can remain."

In short order, the warriors entered the room. Groups of people were herded out, some peacefully, while others had to be beaten over the head with flat swords or prodded forward with shields.

Taking advantage of the distraction, a group of women rushed up and tugged at Darach's tunic to get his attention. One woman spoke for the group, tears streaming down her face. She trembled when he looked at her. "My laird, we've come to beg for food. Our bairns are hungry, our elderly are dying, and yer reply is to have the guardsmen beat and drag us away."

Darach groaned but kept from raising his voice. Already the women shrunk back each time he looked from one to the other. He had given specific instructions that no women be taken out, and no child pushed away. But of course, that would not be the story they told once they returned to their villages.

Even bundled up with cloaks and with blankets around their bodies, it was evident the women were too thin, their faces gaunt, their eyes dull. One held a child against her chest that clung to its mother while crying softly.

"I will not send ye away hungry. Gather all the bairns, women, and any elderly who are here, and go to the dining hall. Food will be brought," Darach said and motioned for his youngest brother Gideon, part of the warrior force, to come forward. "Ensure that Mother and Ella are aware that these people need to be fed."

At eight and twenty, Gideon had turned from a lanky lad into a well-toned, muscled man. With dark wavy hair and the same hazel-colored eyes as him, no one would question his lineage. His brother nodded and raced to find their mother and sister.

"There may be too many to feed on such short notice," Cairn, the councilman, neared and declared. At Darach's glare, he held both hands up. "I only say what I see."

"Go and eat," Darach urged the women who remained in place, looking between him and Cairn. They hurried toward the dining hall, telling others as they walked by to follow them to get a meal.

Most of the women and elderly in the great hall shuffled out, urged by the prospect of a good meal. The few that remained were either quarreling or standing behind their husbands or fathers, who were busy complaining—loudly— about the injustices done against them by Darach's late father.

The argumentative men, who had waited impatiently for him to return, were each given a stipend and sent to see the stablemaster to get a sack of oats each for their livestock.

Another group comprised of four farmers approached and demanded answers on how they were to defend their land. Unfulfilled promises by Darach's late father were repeated.

One man's ragged face contorted with rage. "Laird, we come to ye to ask for help, which has been sorely lacking. For months now, we've struggled to feed our wives and children. Ye must understand, Laird, our land is no longer fertile. Yer late father kept us from rotating the fields, demanding that we plant on all of them at once.

During the last harvest, our farms produced meager crops. After taxes, there was nothing left to take care of our own families."

At a loss as to what should be done for the people who looked to him for answers, Darach scanned the great hall. Too many still remained. Those that had been escorted out by the guards, would return and bring with them more demands for compensation or help.

"Inventory will be done of the grain reserves, ye must give us time," Stuart interjected. "For now, each family will receive two sacks of grain, a pair of sheep, and four chickens."

"There is much to be done. I ask that ye give me time," Darach said meeting each man's gaze. "I am not my father. I wish to work with ye and hear what ye have to say."

The men exchanged questioning looks. One finally spoke. "We will return in a month's time."

"Nay. I will ride out to yer land. For now, prepare the portion of land that ye think will produce the most. Taxes will not be collected until after yer second harvest."

The farmer's faces brightened. "Thank ye, Laird," they said and hurried out to collect their allotments.

Darach leaned toward his scribe. "Mark a reminder to meet with the farmers."

Just then the men who'd been brawling, were dragged up to the front by guardsmen. One was bleeding from his nose and held his head back. The other had a split lip and cut above his eye, blood dripping down the side of his face.

"Laird," one of the guardsmen said. "These men are fighting about poaching." He recognized them. They'd stolen cattle back and forth from each other for years.

Darach studied the men, the one with the bleeding nose was very plump, fat really. A woman, just as plump, stood with him. The other man was healthy and heavy as well. He turned to Stuart. "Where are their lands?"

"Near the river. They share the lands just north of the farmers that were just speaking to ye."

Facing the bleeding men, he studied one and then the other. The room quieted as people became curious to see what happened. "Where do ye get yer grain?"

Confused the men looked at one another. Finally, one replied. "From the miller in the village, like everyone else."

"Ye both have plenty of butter because ye have milk from cows. I presume ye have chickens and sheep as well."

Both nodded.

"Why is everyone around ye hungry?"

His nose had stopped bleeding, so the man looked Darach in the eyes. "I am the provider of meat and milk for the laird. It is I that has had the honor to ensure yer family is well-fed, my laird." The man made a show of bowing.

"What about ye?" Darach asked the other man. "Ye have the same privileges, I presume."

"I do not, my laird," the man replied. "Unlike him." He glared at the other man. "I am an honest man. I am not called to serve my laird, except to provide a yearly tax. I ensure that I feed the families of those that work for me."

Darach looked about the room. "How many here raise livestock?"

A smattering of hands rose and Darach motioned for them to approach. Once the men were lined up, he noted that unlike the two who'd been fighting, the rest of the men were not as plump.

"Every month a different man will provide for the keep and will be paid for it." The men exchanged excited looks. "As far as schedule, ye will meet with my brother Gideon to be assigned a time." Darach hesitated for a beat. "Those in dire need will go first."

The man with the cut above his eye waved his arms. "My laird, if I may be so bold. There are fourteen of us. That means two of us cannot serve ye."

"Neither of ye will serve me for a year," he told the two well-fed men.

The men stared at him with identical gaping wide mouths and eyes, and the wife of one of them swooned.

IT WAS LATE in the day before the crowd in the room had finally thinned enough for last meal to be served.

People had been sent home with enough food and grain to last them for a few weeks. Herders were instructed to gift each family with a goat, sheep, or cow so that they could have milk. Chickens were also distributed.

The council would be discussing how to ensure the clan's homes would be fortified enough for the upcoming cold weather of winter.

Darach stood and stretched. "I need to go for a walk before last meal." Without waiting for anyone to remind him there were still matters that needed to be heard and things which needed to be discussed, he stalked across the room and out the front door.

In the courtyard, people climbed on wagons, and horse-back riders mounted. Other clans people walked to and from a makeshift table where his scribe noted who had been provided with what.

Down the side of the house, there were steps that led to a

lower area. Darach descended the slope and continued down until reaching the shoreline of a loch. At the water's edge, hidden from sight, he lowered to his knees and bent forward covering his face with both hands.

It wasn't as much to pray, but an effort to seek the fortitude to continue. At becoming laird, he'd not been aware of the magnitude of the issues he would face.

Upon his father's death, the truth had come to light of how horrible a leader his father had been. People hadn't come to seek help or guidance for fear of repercussions. Those who had not been in his father's favor now openly complained; the grievances ringing of truth and injustice.

How had he been so blind? Somehow his father had been so controlling of the people that they'd forced smiles and never showed any kind of discord. Now he learned that they were under threat of death for any misdeed his father considered treasonous.

How had it come to be that to ask for food or help was viewed as treason, and therefore, people were on the verge of starvation and death? Those that had livestock and those who grew crops were not allowed to share in case the laird had need of it.

While food rotted in the keep's storehouses, people outside the gates starved.

Fury filled him to the point that screams caught in his throat. Even the soft lapping of the water did little to soothe him.

Senses overwhelmed; all he could do was to take deep breaths and expel them. When his hound caught up with him and lowered to its hunches, Darach reached over and scratched its head. Seeming reassured all was well, the animal rose and began running along the shoreline, picking up a stick and playing.

He watched the dog, jealous over its lack of concern. He'd originally named the black hound Abyss, but in truth, the name did no justice as the animal had a friendly jovial nature. So now he called him Albie.

The cold air swept across the surface of the water bringing with it the smell of the nearby sea. Realizing it had been a long time since he'd allowed himself to just be, he took a deep breath of the salty air.

Stuart, who was the closest to him out of his six siblings, called to him, "Darach, what are ye doing?"

By the way Stuart neared and then followed his line of sight to the loch, his brother needed no explanation.

"Why was Father so cruel to his people?" Darach asked.

"Perhaps he didn't see it as cruelty, but as a way to manage everyone."

Darach studied Stuart. His brother's dark brown hair blowing across the chiseled serious face. "I cannot believe that. We have only to listen to them. To see them. To know how horribly they've been treated."

Stuart straightened his shoulders and held his head high. "We can argue every point of how things have been done in the past. It will not help those people now," he said, motioning toward the house. "What matters right now is that we help them. Set a new standard. Blaze a new trail."

Pushing his shoulder-length blond hair away from his face, Darach met his brother's unwavering gaze. "Only with ye and our family beside me can I do this."

Stuart's lips curved. "With each day that passes, ye become stronger. Ye will be a great leader, Darach. I have little doubt."

"So, a bit of skepticism remains then?" Darach asked with a pointed look.

Stuart returned the look with a lift to his right eyebrow. "Ye are far from perfect, brother. If one were to search for utter perfection, one has to only look at me."

Unable to keep from it, Darach chuckled. Albie, hearing his laugh, raced to him dragging a long branch.

He bent to take the branch from the dog, broke a smaller piece from it, and threw it for the dog to happily retrieve.

"Let us head back."

LAST MEAL IN the family dining room was a quiet affair. In the great hall, the people who had been invited to remain so that their qualms could be heard the following day were fed a simpler fare.

"Duncan and Caelan should be here," Ella, the youngest of the siblings, said, referring to their brothers. "Duncan should be helping ye."

Darach gave her an indulgent look. "They have their own responsibilities in their region. There is the threat from Clan MacNeil and the fact the people there are also revolting upon learning of our father's death.

One of the things Darach was thankful for was that there were seven of them—six brothers and one sister with whom he could divide the burden of what they had been left with.

"What of Clan Uisdein?" Stuart asked, his hazel eyes flashing angrily. "They are refusing to allow me to visit and returned my messenger with threats of harm if we send him back. I am set to marry Fenella Uisdein in the spring."

Gideon let out a bark of laughter. "I would not count on the marriage taking place. She is no doubt relieved, do ye not think?"

Everyone was silent and awaited Stuart's response. Of all the brothers, he had the least fiery temperament, and the possibility of him losing control was low. However, Gideon knew exactly how to goad his brother to anger.

Stuart's chair crashed to the floor when he pushed back. He quickly rounded the table and wrapped his hands around Gideon's neck. "Ye talk too much."

Undaunted by his brother's attack, Gideon punched Stuart in the stomach twice stealing his wind with the second hard punch.

Stuart released Gideon's neck and bent forward blowing out. Just as he was to straighten, Gideon's fist connected with the side of his face.

"Bastard!" Stuart yelled, flying at his younger brother, who tried to flee but failed when Stuart grabbed his tunic.

When both landed on the floor, their mother had had enough. She picked up the pitcher of ale and poured it over them. "Stop this at once."

Lady Mariel Ross was not at all shocked or distressed by her sons' actions. Instead, she returned to her seat and continued eating. She gave Darach a warm look. "I have every trust in ye, son. The obstacles before ye may seem overwhelming but know that ye have the family's support." She slid a look to Stuart and Gideon. "Each and every one of us."

Gideon also returned to his chair to eat, but Stuart, drenched in ale, remained standing. Obviously, their mother knew who needed to cool down.

"I do have news," his mother said in a tone that made his stomach sink. Her face softened. "It isn't anything bad. Perhaps just a bit distressing."

"God's foot, Mother," Ella exclaimed. "Tell us already."

"I received a message today from Lady Macdonald."

"What about?" Darach asked. His mother and Lady Macdonald were childhood friends, both born MacNeil's, they had maintained correspondence even when their husbands were at odds.

"She wishes to visit with me. Either she comes here, or I go there. I know it isn't the best of times, but I do wish for a reprieve."

Darach shook his head. "Ye cannot go there. The Uisdein is threatening our northern shores. I have not heard from the Macdonald in months.

"I do not care," Lady Ross said, lifting her nose. "I will meet with Aileen. She can come here."

"It is much too unstable a time, Mother. If they come here, the Macdonald will learn of the discord with our people. He could use the information against us."

Stuart spoke next. "Ye cannot travel there, we cannot afford to lose the guardsmen to escort ye right now."

When Lady Ross and Ella exchanged looks, Darach let out a groan.

"What?" Gideon asked. "Why are ye making a sound of pain."

"Do ye not see it?" Darach asked. "Lady Macdonald is

already traveling here. Am I correct, Mother?" He glared at his mother.

"Arrangements were made. I couldn't very well tell her not to come."

He let out a long breath not wishing to yell. "Ye very well could have."

His mother brightened. "This is actually the perfect time for ye to get to know her daughter Beatrice, who comes with her. A marriage between our clans would be very beneficial."

Laird for only half a year, he'd not had time to think of much more than the mountain of troubles his father had left him with.

"It took me this long to convince the clan they would not be punished for bringing their issues to me. I still have to work on what is needed for the villagers, farmers, and guardsmen. I am much too busy to begin to consider marriage." Darach shook his head.

Stuart, who'd calmed, lowered to a chair. "Besides, we should concentrate on my marriage."

"I am not sure we should align with Clan Uisdein as yet. Not until I understand where their loyalties lay." Darach met his brother's gaze. "Be patient."

Stuart nodded; his jaw tight.

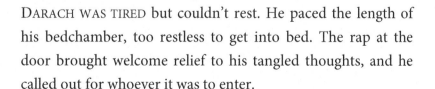

DARACH WAS TIRED but couldn't rest. He paced the length of his bedchamber, too restless to get into bed. The rap at the door brought welcome relief to his tangled thoughts, and he called out for whoever it was to enter.

Upon the door opening and the woman entering, Darach considered what to do. In truth, he was in no mood for lovemaking. The woman Lilia had often shared his bed, but as of late, their times together had become less and less frequent.

"My laird." Lilia neared, her gaze sliding down his body. "Today has been most tiring for ye, has it not?"

"It was. But I am not sure I want to be…" He stopped talking when Lilia's hand clutched his shaft through the fabric of his breeches.

Immediately his body responded, ready for relief in whatever form it came.

"Lilia…I cannot possibly satisfy ye today," Darach said despite obviously going hard, the rest of his body felt as if stones were tied to his ankles and hung from his wrists.

"Allow me to put ye to bed then," the woman cooed. Lilia was well versed in seeing to a man's needs and had been his lover for the last year.

He was sure she slept with others but Darach turned a blind eye, as he didn't care what she did when not with him. The way he saw it, Lilia was intelligent enough to know he would never offer marriage. Other than ensuring she was provided for, he allowed her freedom.

Voluptuous, with waist length brown hair, Lilia was enticing. Her almond shaped eyes that lifted at the outer corners, gave her an exotic look. She poured water into a pot by the fireplace and turned the lever so that it hovered over the fire to warm.

Taking Darach's hand, Lilia guided him to sit on the bed and then kneeled to remove his boots and stockings. "Ye should not allow yerself to become so exhausted. There are others who could shoulder some of yer burden."

Darach nodded. "Ye are correct, but as laird I must see to all my responsibilities."

As she often did, Lilia preferred to distract him from worries of the day, so she smiled, her plump lips then pursed and motioned for him to hold his arms up.

She made quick work dispensing with his tunic and breeches until he was completely naked.

"Just a moment," Lilia said. Then she went to the hearth and returned with a bowl of warm water. She grabbed a thick piece of cloth and dipped it into the bowl. She wiped his face, arms, legs, and chest. Purposely waiting until last to cleanse his midsection.

"Lay upon the bed, Laird," she instructed, and Darach did. While she saw to his thighs and hips, his eyes became heavy.

However, when she began to wash his sex, his breath hitched, and there was little he could do to avoid getting hard again.

"Ye are good to me," he murmured.

Her wet hands slid up and down his shaft until he got even harder. "I see ye need relief, my laird," Lilia purred, her lips tightening over the tip of his sex, then she took him fully into her mouth. It wasn't long before he came, his head pushed back into the bedding at the release.

If he was tired before, now he was spent.

Sprawled naked on the bed, the cool air of the room fanned over his heated body, and he realized he had no desire to move. Lilia pulled a blanket over him and pressed a kiss to his cheek.

"Sleep well, my laird," she whispered in his ear and left.

CHAPTER TWO

"MUST I GO?" Isobel Macdonald asked her mother, who flittered about her parent's huge bedchamber directing servants to pack enough gowns and shoes as if they were traveling to visit royalty.

Lady Macdonald looked at her, patience radiating from her gaze. "Do not forget yer gift for Ella, Isobel." She then turned to the door. "Where is Beatrice?"

"She is packing," Isobel said, annoyed at not being heard. "Mother, I would prefer to remain here. I have much to do and there is no reason for me to go. It is Beatrice who Father wishes to marry off to a Ross."

Her mother looked at her as if she were daft. "There are three other single brothers who would make a good husband for ye. Due to yer unfortunate situation, we cannot offer ye to the new laird, but the next eldest, Duncan, I believe would make a good match for ye."

Isobel tried a new tactic. "Father is not going; therefore, I should remain with him. What if he becomes unwell? He will certainly be thankful for one of us to remain here to care for him."

"One of yer brothers can take care of him."

"It is not the same and ye know it."

Her mother wrinkled her nose in thought and Isobel became hopeful.

"No, ye will go. I will ensure Maura looks after yer father," she replied, referring to the housekeeper.

Rounding her shoulders, Isobel gave up, walked out of the bedchamber and headed down the corridor to her own. It was smaller than Beatrice's, but she'd chosen it because in her opinion this room had a much better view.

From her window, she could see both the forest and a small inlet along which birlinns were lined up ready to be sailed off to sea, or in most cases across the inlet to the Isle of Harris.

Annis, her maid, hurried in dragging a small trunk. "Miss Isobel, yer mother said ye get only a small trunk as there willna be room since she and Miss Beatrice have packed so much already."

It didn't matter to her since she rarely took time with her appearance. Isobel had no desire to court or to marry anytime soon. Her plans were many as yet, only a very special man could convince her away.

"I forgot to ask Mother how long we will remain. Do ye know?"

Annis nodded. "I believe we are to stay for the remainder of the summer season."

"I cannot possibly be gone that long. Father needs me," Isobel grumbled.

"Just a few weeks is all," Annis, ever cheerful, replied. "It will be a nice change."

"I suppose," Isobel said. "We must pack my sketchbooks, pencils, and chalks. It will give me something to do."

It did not take long for her packing to be done as she only

took four dresses, two nightgowns, and a few undergarments. Other than a brush, mirror, and a set of ribbons, she had no need to pack more. It was best not to stand out, as her sister was who her parents planned to marry off.

Leaving Annis to continue sorting through her things to ensure it all fit in the small trunk, Isobel rushed out to the great hall. They were not to leave until the next day, which gave her a few more hours to plead her case against traveling.

In the great hall, she found her father. He no longer sat at the high board, but in a wide chair that was made comfortable with blankets. His feet were elevated on a footstool that had been fashioned for comfort. As he watched over the day's activities, he lazily ran his hand over a large orange cat on his lap. Although afflicted by an ailment that kept him from moving about easily, her father remained clear of mind and continued to lord over the clan. With light brown eyes, and a trim gray beard that covered his square jaw, he remained attractive.

At seeing her, his lips curved, and he motioned for her to come sit next to him. Her eldest brother, Evander, shook his head, obviously annoyed at the interruption.

She waited as the council discussed the upcoming harvest and division of duties. It was a mundane daily activity that had always fascinated her.

"Should ye not be seeing about the midday meal?" Evander whispered in her ear.

Isobel gave him a droll look. "Should ye not be out somewhere sticking yer sword in a straw dummy?" The double entendre was meant to annoy him as he was currently embroiled in a situation with two women, both of whom were demanding his attention. It was not the first time.

Their father had become too lenient as his illness progressed. Evander should be married and settled by now, but he had managed to talk their father out of ordering him to do so.

"What is on yer mind daughter?" her father asked when the council finally took a break from the discussion.

She leaned into his ear. "May I remain here with ye and not go with Mother and Beatrice to visit Clan Ross?" She didn't give him an opportunity to reply before continuing, "Ye will be left alone, and I should be here to keep ye company."

"Aye, ye should," he said with a teasing grin. "However, yer mother told me that if ye came to me, I should remain firm in our decision that ye must go."

"It is Beatrice who will garner the new laird's attention. One look upon her beauty and he will not hesitate to agree to marriage."

Laird Macdonald studied her for a long moment. "Do ye not have a looking glass Isobel? Yes, yer sister is quite bonnie, but ye are as beautiful. It is not because of her looks that we present her for marriage."

"I know Father," Isobel said, quick to reassure him. "I am not bitter about it. It is no one's fault that I cannot be first choice."

Evander huffed, his two-colored eyes flashing angrily. "It certainly is someone's fault, and that bastard is lucky to still be alive." Her brother was a handsome younger version of their father. The main difference were Evander's eyes. The right one brown like their father, the left hazel, like their mother. Despite the curious feature, it did not keep lasses of all ages from seeking a tumble with him. And he rarely turned them down. Which was one of the reasons he found himself in a tangle of two women demanding his attention.

Not sure how much he'd overheard, Isobel turned to her brother. "Mother says either ye or Padraig will take care of Father while we are gone. I am trying to convince Father to allow me to remain. I know ye are both much too busy."

Her brother's eyes narrowed, and he stroked his chin in thought. "Maura will stay behind, will she not?"

The battle was lost. Isobel gave up trying to come up with another argument. She was to go to South Uist, the home of a new laird she barely remembered.

"I require yer help," Beatrice said as soon as Isobel entered her sister's room. Gowns, shifts, and other various articles of clothing were strewn everywhere. On the floor, next to the two trunks, sat Annis looking quite defeated.

The room was bright because the balcony doors were open allowing sunlight to stream inside. Her sister's blond hair was loose, framing her heart-shaped face with a riot of curls, making her look like a wild fae on a quest.

"Whatever are ye doing?" Isobel asked lifting a gown from the floor and inspecting it for tears. "Ye must allow Annis to complete the packing. We leave first thing in the morning."

Her sister sank onto the bed and fell back, blending into the piles of clothing. "I do not wish to go. I do not wish to marry the ogre."

"Why do ye say that?" Isobel neared the bed, lifted a pile of clothes and placed them atop one of the trunks. She nodded at Annis, signaling that the servant should pack them.

Immediately, Beatrice began to cry. "Because he is terrifying. Ye did not go with Mother and me last time we visited. Ye should have seen him, he is like a wild beast. Huge and overwhelming."

Isobel did her best to imagine the slender blond young man she'd met years earlier and could not fathom he would have changed so much.

"Darach was quite kind to us when he visited last. He whittled a horse and gifted it to me."

Beatrice sat up and glared, her beauty not marred by the expression. "That was over ten years ago Isobel. Ye have no idea how much he has changed. He is not the same person. His brothers are just as beastly. They are all huge and bulky."

"Evander is huge and bulky," Isobel said softly. "He is not scary."

"Yes he is," Beatrice insisted, her blue eyes glistening. "Not to us because we are used to him, but to others, they find him quite intimidating."

Thinking back to the last visit by Lady Ross, the sons who'd accompanied her, Stuart and Gideon, had been large men, who'd gotten along well with Evander and Padraig. She'd not had any opportunity to spend time with either one, as they'd kept their distance from her and Beatrice.

"I do admit to them being large men, but Gideon was playful."

Annis came to the bed and pulled a gown from under Beatrice's leg. Her sister didn't protest, but watched silently, as the servant completed the task of packing.

"Tell me why do ye not wish to marry," Isobel prodded. "Are ye truly fearful of Darach Ross, or of marrying?"

A warm breeze blew into the room, and for a moment, Isobel closed her eyes, enjoying the remainder of the beautiful day outside. Instead of packing and fretting with Beatrice, she wished to be outside sketching and capturing the beauty of nature.

"I do not care for him in the least. He scares me. I would rather marry a gentler man," Beatrice replied. "It is unfair that we do not get a choice in the matter of who we are to spend the rest of our lives with."

Isobel took her sister's hand. "Come let us go for a walk. The fresh air will do ye good."

Indeed, Beatrice's countenance changed once they walked out into the field that surrounded their home. They avoided the side where the guards split their time between training and resting and went the opposite way.

"I will collect flowers to place on our table for last meal," Beatrice said. and seeming to forget her troubles, she began to pick blooms.

The picture of her sister, hair flying in the wind, the golden waves circling about her delicate face made Isobel want to cry. Beatrice was much too delicate to be married to a beastly man. Surely her mother would change her mind upon seeing him again.

"Pick some flowers," Beatrice called out. Isobel plucked a few as she considered what needed to be done. Somehow, she would try to find the young man that she'd gotten to know those many years ago. He had to exist inside the man Darach was now. Hopefully, she could appeal to his good nature and dissuade him from marrying Beatrice.

In the distance, a cart laden with crates ambled by along a road that led to the nearby village. She recognized the peddler who often came to the keep offering his wares to the servants, the guardsmen, and the family as well.

Following the wagon's progress, she was sad to have missed his visit. With all the packing and such, she'd not been aware he'd come. Beatrice straightened upon catching sight of the peddler and stomped her foot. "Why did I not know he came today?"

Maura had not told them, probably ordered by their mother not to.

"I am sure Mother did not wish us distracted from preparing for our trip," Isobel replied, letting out a sigh. "There will sure to be other peddlers when we visit Ross Lands. They may have items we've not seen before."

"Very true," Beatrice's lips curved. "We will have ribbons and other things that none of my friends have. They will be envious."

Not wishing to draw attention to the fact that Beatrice would not be seeing her friends any time soon, if she did indeed marry Darach, Isobel sought to distract her. "It would be nice if ye brought them back gifts instead, then they'd be more excited to see ye."

"Hmm," Beatrice murmured to herself as she considered her suggestion. By the look of doubt, Isobel knew her sister would do no such thing. It wasn't that Beatrice was boastful. On the contrary, her sister was sweet and caring. Though, for whatever reason, she surrounded herself with young women who were superficial and uncaring of others. The main focus of their conversations seemed to focus on flirtation, hair styling, and making themselves appealing to men. Most of them were to be married in the next year or two, so they were focused on finding a desirable husband. Not unlike Beatrice, most of them would be matched by their families to a man who would bring some kind of advantage.

It was a very few who actually got to pick, but it didn't stop the young women from their quests. In a way, Isobel found it endearing. Though more times than not, she considered their inability to accept reality annoying.

"Ye should have had a new gown made," Beatrice said, interrupting her train of thought.

"It is ye who has to stand out, sister. I have packed good, serviceable clothing that will serve me well," Isobel responded.

Beatrice was not to be deterred. "Ye will wear some of mine. Mother wishes to find a husband for ye as well. The drab dresses ye insist on wearing will not do in the least."

"I am much taller than ye and would look ridiculous in one of yer dresses." Isobel laughed when Beatrice made a face, realizing she was right.

"Oh no," her sister said, looking down at Isobel's dress. "We must hurry back inside. I am going to ensure at least a pair of nice gowns are packed for ye." Despite Isobel not wishing to waste time on clothing she would not require, she allowed her sister to drag her back inside.

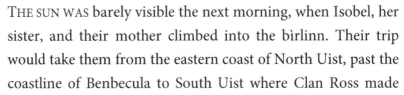

THE SUN WAS barely visible the next morning, when Isobel, her sister, and their mother climbed into the bìrlinn. Their trip would take them from the eastern coast of North Uist, past the coastline of Benbecula to South Uist where Clan Ross made their home.

It would be an entire day of travel in the vessel with eight rowers and three men who manned the bìrlinn. Most of the trip would hopefully be done by sail, but in case it was not possible the rowers would take over.

Settled into their seats at the back of the bìrlinn, under a thick covering that was made to give privacy, Isobel held a journal on her lap, her fingers rubbing across the top of the leatherbound book as she peered out a side opening. Her home became smaller and smaller as they sailed away, and she prayed for her father and brothers that they remain safe.

Her mother met her gaze. "I am glad ye came. Too long ye have remained cloistered at the keep, rarely venturing farther than the walls."

"I am happy with my simple way of life, Mother," Isobel insisted. "Ye worry for naught. I promise to be content with my life."

With a dubious look, her mother let out a sigh. "I believe that ye believe it, Isobel. However, ye used to hope for so much more. To travel and see other lands, to find beautiful places to sketch, and ye ached for a family."

Angry words sprung to her lips and yet somehow Isobel managed to keep them from sprouting forth. "Everyone has the same desires. To experience, to explore, and to love. But not everyone will achieve them. It is the reality of life."

"I wish to live in a beautiful home, married to a handsome young man, who indulges me," Beatrice quipped. "I will inform Darach Ross of this upon meeting him."

"Beatrice, ye must not say anything of that nature," Lady Macdonald replied. "I forbid it. Ye must be amicable and hold only a light conversation."

"How will that help them get to know one another if the

only subject that is allowed will be the weather?" Isobel quipped. "I would certainly wish to know him better and see if we were compatible. It is important to know what his expectations are."

"That comes in due course," their mother replied while pinching the bridge of her nose. "I must rest. We shall speak about this more at another time."

Beatrice and Isobel exchanged a knowing look. Their mother had hoped the subject would be dropped permanently.

"I have an idea," Isobel told her sister, once she assessed that their mother was asleep.

"What is it?" Beatrice asked, with a curious expression.

"Since ye will not be allowed to ask Darach Ross direct questions, what if I do it for ye?"

Beatrice started to clap but stopped before her hands collided and looked to their mother. "I have a better idea," she said, keeping her voice down in case their mother stirred. "Ye must tell Laird Ross that I have no desire to marry him. Or anyone else for that matter. Not as yet."

It was doubtful there was anything Isobel could say to the man that would put him off marrying her beautiful sister. She certainly could not aspire to draw his attention away.

Today, Beatrice's hair had been pulled back into a long braid. The braid was then wrapped about her head and pinned in place. Ribbons were added to stabilize it. Even a sea storm would have no effect on Beatrice's hairstyle. Dressed in a dark blue velvet gown that brought out the blue of her eyes, she appeared to be royalty.

Isobel peered down at her plain muslin brown dress and knew she would instantly blend into the background when compared to her sister.

However, if he was to court Beatrice, the best she could do would be to ensure that Darach Ross was a good match for her.

The bìrlinn cut through the water easily, the sea was calm this day, and Isobel was grateful for it. Despite living by the sea, she preferred to travel over land. However, it wasn't possible to go to another isle other than by bìrlinn.

Moments later everyone including Annis had fallen asleep, Isobel pulled a blanket over her companions and looked across the water to the second bìrlinn that accompanied them. On that one was mostly guardsmen and their trunks. She huffed annoyed that her chalks and sketchbook were packed. The view of the other vessel would have made for a nice rendering.

The sun was warm, the smell of the salty air and the breeze provided a perfect setting to lull one to sleep. But Isobel could not rest. Her mind kept going over what Beatrice has said, that Darach Ross had somehow morphed into a beastly angry man. They lived too far away to know much about the circumstances of what happened at Clan Ross. The late laird had left behind a powerful legacy. Their army was large, their lands vast, and from what she recalled, the keep where the family lived was enormous and quite beautiful.

She leaned against the side of the boat and gazed out to where the cloudless sky and the sea met. Perhaps one day she would find a way to travel, to see many things. If nothing else, this was an opportunity to explore new surroundings and become reacquainted with Ella, the youngest of the Ross siblings.

After all, Isobel had freedoms Beatrice did not. Since her parents were not in any particular hurry to marry her off, she could afford the luxury of enjoying her visit.

CHAPTER THREE

F ROM WHERE DARACH stood atop a hill, he could see far out to sea. In the distance, two bìrlinns came into view. He signaled with his arms letting those below know. Deciding to remain above the others, he wished to get a good look at the visitors before riding down to the shoreline.

Only Lady Macdonald and her two daughters were to arrive, along with eight or ten guardsmen and a servant. The Macdonald bìrlinns would return to North Uist after a day of rest, so the accompanying men would be hosted at the keep for two nights.

Despite what his mother said, this was more than a trip for two old friends to get together. The reason for the visit was for him to get to know Beatrice Macdonald and become betrothed. From what he remembered from her last visit, she was beautiful and somewhat fragile looking. The young woman had done her best to avoid him, and the one time they'd been accidentally alone, she'd acted as if he would eat her alive.

It mattered not to him if a woman was astoundingly gorgeous. If she was not at ease around him, then he could not bear to take such a woman as a wife.

There was an older sister, Isobel. He recalled that when barely ten and nine, he'd considered himself enamored of her. She would be visiting as well. However, she was not offered to him to marry. One of the first things he wanted to know was why.

Although it had been quite a few years since seeing her, they had gotten along quite well. Perhaps she was already betrothed. Her mother had mentioned something about a betrothal. It would have been better, in his estimation, to have the option of Isobel over Beatrice.

When the birlinns reached the shore, he urged his steed forward, the animal eager to get to the water, galloped down the side of the hill until upon the shore's edge.

It was an unnaturally warm day and despite the breeze, he didn't like the feel of his long hair down the back of his neck, so he pulled a leather strap from his saddlebag to tie it back.

He dismounted and allowed his horse to roam along the water, meanwhile with the strap between his teeth, he used both hands to sweep up the hair, then tied it.

For a moment he took in what happened. The women were helped from the birlinn, each one stepping onto the moor. All four carried something, one had a pillow, two held small bags, and another, who he assumed was the servant by her drab clothing, clutched what looked to be a journal.

They were greeted with hugs by his mother and sister, while he and Gideon were held back ensuring the trunks were all loaded onto the waiting wagon.

When his mother motioned for him to come closer, Darach held up a hand and signaled to his horse.

Gideon looked at him. "Are we to go meet them now?"

"Ye can if ye wish, I have to get my horse. There will be time enough to meet them back at the keep."

His brother shrugged. "True."

Once mounted, he and Gideon rode in front of the procession that would take them through a village to their home. It was not a long trip, perhaps an hour, but it was long enough that he brought twenty men as a show of force and a warning to any threats.

He did not take time to speak to anyone, but the murmur of the women's conversation floated in the air to his ears.

Even though he wasn't sure he cared to marry, Darach could not deny that he liked the sound of women's voices. The familiar ones of Ella and his mother's mixed with four new ones. A particular throaty voice sounded familiar, and he wondered if it was Isobel. He recognized Beatrice right away, her hair braided wrapped tightly around her head did not distract from the young woman's beauty. And yet he had not noticed which one was Isobel.

"Do ye think Duncan and Caelan will be at the house?" Gideon asked.

Darach had sent a messenger to ensure all was well and received a curt reply that they would come if their duties allowed.

"If they are not, I will go to them. Hopefully, they are not trying to handle a situation alone that requires our help."

His brother looked in the direction of the estate where their brothers lived. "It is possible the people of the village there have the same complaints as those that come to see ye here."

The rest of the way Darach became more and more annoyed at his brothers. If neither Duncan nor Caelan were at the keep when they arrived, he would leave first thing the next morning and have a serious conversation with them. Just because they lived in a different home did not mean they could ignore him—their laird.

Once the party entered the gates, Darach dismounted and waited for the carriage to stop. The women had insisted on riding together in the tight space. He expected they'd be overheated in such a small, cramped area.

A guard hurried to the door to open it and sure enough when his sister popped out her face was flushed and reddened. Darach let out a breath. Women were strange creatures.

ALTHOUGH THE CONVERSATION had been enjoyable, Isobel could hardly wait to get out of the cramped hot carriage. Lady Ross had insisted they always took one carriage in order to spend the first hour talking without the interruption of men. It seemed her mother was in agreement although both older women looked about ready to faint.

While the older women sat with a miserable Annis squashed against the side, talking the entire time, Isobel and Beatrice had enjoyed Ella's non-stop chatter.

It was as if the Ross women were starved for female company.

Isobel had tried, without success, to ask about Ella's older brother, but she'd been non-committal in her replies.

"He has a lot of responsibility on his shoulders at the moment," was her reply to his temperament. And "Darach enjoys walks alone," when she asked about his hobbies.

After the long ride to the keep, she'd not acquired any information to help in her quest to dissuade the man from marrying Beatrice.

After the older women exited the carriage, Annis fell sideways onto the seat. Her dramatics making both Isobel and Beatrice giggle.

Isobel allowed Beatrice to exit first as she was who should get the attention. After her sister was assisted down by a large man, Isobel was assisted down by a guard, who looked past her to the interior of the carriage. Looking over her shoulder, she saw Annis straighten and give the guard an eye roll.

"There ye go miss," the guard said, leading her to the party that awaited her.

She kept her gaze down as Annis hurried to catch up. "Miss Isobel, I will see about unpacking and such."

"No, ye will come with me and see about getting something to drink and eat," Isobel said, pulling Annis forward by the arm. "Ye are as tired as we are. Come with me."

Upon approaching the group, everyone walked inside. Darach stood beside a guardsman, who held the door open for them.

When Isobel looked to him, he met her gaze for only a beat. Her breath quickened at noting how very different he was. Beatrice had not exaggerated.

Darach had grown at least a head since she last saw him, and the span of his shoulders and chest must have doubled. His eyes were a color she couldn't quite place. They seemed to go from green to blue. He looked between her and Annis and frowned but did not say anything.

Once in a large room, which she assumed was the great hall by its size, they walked to the front of the room where four men and one woman stood.

Lady Ross smiled at them and hurried to the line of people who waited. "It always lightens my heart to see all my children together," she exclaimed.

"Her children are quite grown," Annis mumbled, and Isobel pressed her lips together to keep from smiling.

Ella motioned to the men. "Isobel since ye have not seen my brothers in many years I will reintroduce ye." She motioned to the first man. "This is my second eldest brother, Duncan." She continued down the line. "This is Stuart, Ewan, and our youngest brother Gideon." Each man nodded in acknowledgment in her direction.

Ella pulled a pretty woman forward. "This is Catriona, Ewan's wife."

Isobel smiled at the woman, liking her immediately.

"Do I not get introduced?" Darach grumbled walking to stand in front of his siblings, his gaze moved from her to Beatrice and finally to Annis.

Ella came to stand next to him, seeming to become shorter, "My brother and Laird Ross, Darach."

"It is nice to see ye again. I still have the horse ye made me," Isobel said.

When his gaze scanned over her, he did so in a cursory dismissive way. He then looked to Beatrice and her mother.

If he was comparing them, Isobel was sure he wondered how they could be sisters. In truth, they were so very different. Beatrice, a perfect delicate-looking creature; then her, a swan just before transforming.

"I am glad to hear it," he finally responded. He didn't look glad at all. If anything, he seemed bothered. Isobel and Annis took a step backward when he looked to them again.

He finally went to her mother and Beatrice. "Welcome to our home," Darach said bowing over Beatrice's hand, who visibly shook. Her eyes widened and she turned to Isobel as if asking for rescue. When he moved to their mother, Beatrice took a step away.

There was little Isobel could do for her sister at that moment. Especially when he invited everyone to eat and offered his arms to both Beatrice and her mother.

Catriona came up to her. "I know ye must be exhausted. We shall not linger over the meal and allow ye to plenty of time rest in yer bedchambers."

"Thank ye," Isobel said. "I am very tired, and also a bit hungry. I would appreciate the rest but expect Mother will remain up with Lady Ross visiting."

Once in the dining room, everyone found a seat. Beatrice hurried to the opposite end of the table, away from Darach, and sat. Isobel looked side to side unsure where to sit.

"Sit next to me," Catriona said, pulling her to the last chair on one side. Isobel wanted to groan out loud when Darach lowered to sit on her right.

"Isobel, ye have changed a great deal since I saw ye last," he remarked. By the expression on his face, he did not mean it as a compliment. Actually, it was hard to tell how he meant it as he had a pretty blank look.

Doing her best to imitate him, she retorted, "Ye look quite different as well."

Other than nod, he looked down the table to his mother.

Isobel couldn't help but smile at seeing identical beaming expressions between her mother and Lady Ross.

"They are so happy when together," Isobel said while still

looking at them.

Catriona nodded. "Lady Ross has spoken of nothing else than the visit. She was anxious for her arrival."

"They are childhood friends, who adore each other," Isobel said. She did her best not to look to her right because she sensed Darach was studying her. A part of her wanted to speak to him, to begin the dialog that would hopefully take them to the point of her feeling comfortable enough to speak of Beatrice. However, at the moment she was tired and sure to look disheveled from the travel.

"Did ye have a smooth sail, Miss Isobel?" one of the brothers asked. She wasn't quite sure of his name, but she guessed him to be Catriona's husband Ewan by the way he looked at the pretty woman.

"It was quite comfortable. The seas cooperated perfectly. My only complaint was that I left my sketchbook and chalks in my trunk, so I could not capture the scenery."

"Remarkable," Catriona said. "Perhaps ye can sketch our bairn." She smiled at the man across from her. Isobel had guessed right. He was Ewan, the fourth born brother.

Unable to keep from it, she slid a glance to the silent man beside her. He was certainly handsome and would make a good subject for a sketch. Every line of his face strong and prominent, from the square jawline to his slender nose. The shape of his mouth, surely it looked better when his lips were not pressed together so tightly.

Isobel fought to keep from looking at his eyes and realized she'd been studying him, while he glared at her. "Do ye have any hobbies, Laird?"

His brows lowered further. "I do not."

Biting her lower lip to keep from telling him he was not good company, Isobel turned away. She had absolutely no reason to mind her manners or try to befriend the angry man. Each of the brothers, to a certain degree, could be seen as intimidating. Each of them was broad of chest, tall, and quite muscular. However, none of them came across as being in as foul a mood as the eldest.

Beatrice had not been wrong.

Darach Ross was a beastly man.

CHAPTER FOUR

T HE ABANDONED HOUSE made a perfect place for the group to meet in secret. Hidden by not only a thick patch of woods but also walls on three sides, those that gathered did not worry about being found out.

Cairn McKinney held up a lantern and inspected the faces of the men there. He cleared his throat and wondered if they were all loyal to the cause or there out of curiosity. At the moment, it mattered little. The insurgent movement was new; he'd just begun planning for a way to overthrow the new laird and become the new leader of the people.

"Too many of us are hungry and dying," someone in the group called out. "We must do something."

"Take the lands from the Ross, take the keep for ourselves," another added.

In truth, he had no desire to share much with them. Sure, at first when they helped him become the leader. But once he had all the power, then he'd order the guards to imprison anyone who went against him.

His lips curved. As a council member and a trusted advisor who sat at the right of the new laird, he was perfectly positioned for what had to be done. Already he'd begun by ensuring people crowded the great hall daily, bringing with them petty complaints and making demands. The young laird was growing tired and overwhelmed.

Soon he would be easy to control. And if not, then he would die, perhaps in a terrible manner that would claim the life of one or two of his brothers as well.

A man, who served as a guard for the laird, and was a particularly prized recruit shook his head. "There are six brothers, this quest of ours has to be better planned."

"I am well aware," Cairn snapped. "This is only the beginning."

"How is this going to put food in my bairns' bellies?" a farmer mumbled. "We cannot wait until winter."

After hours of discussions that at times turned into screaming matches, there was no cohesive plan. Not outwardly. His main objective had been reached, the men were angry and turning against the Ross family. Most of the useless men in the room right then were poor and with no vision other than to have food and shelter.

He had to find someone intelligent, but easy for him to manipulate, to help him from inside. He studied the guardsman. He would be useful. But there was another person, whom he had to persuade.

"I must ask that we end the evening. Our plan today is to consider the best way to find more men to come to our side. This must be done without alerting the Ross family. Ye must be discreet in yer search. Find out first if they are angry toward the laird."

The guard looked around the room. "Do not tell anyone about this meeting place. It is not the time for it yet."

With a somewhat clear plan, the men in the room settled. That's what they needed Cairn decided, some sort of goal.

"The best time for the insurrection will be late fall. By winter, we will be in the keep."

The men cheered, although admittedly, some looked dubious. Cairn made a mental note to speak to each of those that looked less than convinced alone. He didn't need anyone to go running to the family just because they didn't agree with his ideals.

As the men filed out, most of them giving him nods of acknowledgment and reinforcing their alliance, Cairn pulled one man aside. "Seamus, I am surprised to see ye here. I thought ye loyal to the laird."

"As of late, I have grown disillusioned. The late laird, rest his soul, was not perfect, but he gave me favor. That son of his looks down his nose at me." His arm swept across the room. "At all of us."

"I will see ye in a fortnight then." Cairn watched the men file out, then walked out into the darkness to catch up with a farmer, who he doubted was there for the right reasons.

"Will ye return for our next gathering?" he asked the man when he reached him.

The farmer shook his head. "This is not for me. I do not wish to harm anyone. I thought we were going to come up with a plan to approach the laird with—a way for our families to flourish."

Cairn put his arm around the man's shoulders. "That sort of thing keeps us in our place, no one's situation will change."

The man gave him a confused look. "It is the way of things. A leader for the clan, someone to rule the people. Nothing we do will change that. Either Laird Ross or ye, it will not matter who is in charge, the rest of us will not see much of a difference."

Eyes widened in surprise when Cairn sunk the blade into the man's side. When realization struck it was too late, Cairn stabbed him again. The farmer crumpled to the ground and Cairn leaned over him. "Yer right, I will be the new clan's leader. However, ye will not live to see that day."

Cairn hurried back to the empty house, found his steed, and mounted. Deciding it was best to be seen just in case there were questions regarding the man's death, Cairn urged his horse in the direction of the village tavern.

CHAPTER FIVE

T HE NEXT DAY, Darach broke his fast in his bedchamber, not in the mood to be around people. The great hall would soon be overcrowded again, and the dining room was filled with his mother's visitors, who would be chatting the day away as if they've not a care in the world.

It was not fair to be so angered by his mother's visitors. She did have plans for the group to do things for the poor. What bothered him was that there was so much to do, so many problems to take care of. The last thing he needed was for his mother to be playing matchmaker at a time like this.

If he was to marry, the arrangement did not need to include him at any level. He would choose a woman, and as far as he was concerned, his mother and whoever else could take care of the rest. Silly that they thought he could take time at the moment to court.

"Laird, the council waits," his valet stood by the door, the older man's eyes scanning over him. "Do ye plan to dress today?"

Putting down his cup, Darach gave him his best glare. "No, Ramey, I plan to stroll about the keep naked."

Ramey had worked for their family for decades. The older man had become Darach's valet after a heated argument between the valet and his father. The only reason his father had not sent the man away, was because the man had been in the family's service since a young lad.

"What do ye think about our recent visitors, Ramey?" Darach began as he allowed the man to help him dress. "Mother thinks I should marry the flowery creature that has been floating about the keep since yesterday."

"Yer mother is correct in that it is past time for ye and yer brothers to marry. All of ye, except for Gideon, are over thirty years of age."

"There is no time limit for marriage."

"Most lasses prefer to marry someone that is attractive and has all their teeth," Ramey replied with a stern expression.

Darach slid him a side glance. "What of the lass? I know ye have an opinion."

"Is it not yer opinion that counts most?"

Sitting down to don his boots, Darach nodded. "The sister, Isobel. She dresses like a servant. I actually thought her to be one. Her dress is drab as if she does not wish to garner any attention. She seems the more intelligent and far more beautiful of the two."

"Then marry the drab dressing one," Ramey said. "Do not complicate things."

Darach's lips curved. The man had a way of setting things straight.

UPON ENTERING THE great hall, there were not as many people about like the day before. He stopped to speak to a group of sheepherders, who were there to complain about land distribution. Darach called to Stuart, who along with a group of guardsmen, had been riding out to inspect the lands.

"Ride out with these men and review their land allotments. Ensure they each have the same quarter that buts up to the river."

Stuart studied each man in turn with so much intensity that they began to shrink back. "I was just there, speaking to ye less than seven days ago. What has changed?"

"Nothing, sir," one finally said. "We were told to come and ensure the laird agreed."

Darach whirled to the group and shouted. "My brother's word is my word. Do not ever question it." He curled his hands into fists. "If anyone here brings up something that my brothers have already given a decision on, I will throw ye in the dungeon."

The room emptied.

Stuart pressed his lips together and gave him a droll look. "That worked." His gaze moved past Darach to a doorway and he turned to find Isobel standing there, her journal in hand, eyes wide.

"I suppose her father doesn't threaten his people with a dungeon first thing in the morning," Stuart quipped.

Darach let out a breath. The last thing he needed were delicate creatures that had to be coddled every other moment.

Just then a woman dragging a child behind rushed past him. She grabbed a man who stood by the doorway. "Ye have nothing important to tell the laird. He is much too busy for yer whining."

Darach frowned while unsure what to do.

The family hurried out.

Then to his surprise, laughter rang out.

Isobel was laughing so hard, she had to wipe tears from her

eyes. "Oh, my goodness, this is the most entertainment I've had in years."

She walked into the great hall and turned in a circle. "Ye managed to run off even the dog."

"My dog is probably in the kitchen," Darach grumbled.

Stuart went to Isobel. "What do ye have in that book of yers?"

When she smiled at his brother, she transformed, becoming even more beautiful. "I write my thoughts. Although, for the most part, I have to save my thought until later, since I do not carry ink and quill. But it gives me comfort to hold it."

He was about to ask her about her choice of dress but couldn't find a way to word so that it would not be insulting. Just then his mother and the other women appeared.

They descended the stairs as Darach walked back toward the kitchens.

"Darach," his mother called out.

"I must find Albie," he said, turning on his heel and hurrying away.

ONCE HE FOUND his dog—who was, in fact, in the kitchen—he and the animal went out the side door to where the guardsmen practiced. Already warriors warmed up by swinging their swords with one arm and then the other.

They were learning the trick of tossing the sword from one hand to the other and completing mirror maneuvers. His brother Ewan, who'd returned from mainland Scotland, taught them the motions. Ewan stood in front of several men, explaining how it worked as the men tried to do it. Many times, swords fell to the ground; other times, the men managed to catch it but could not complete the motions.

Darach strolled to where the men were and watched as Ewan demonstrated several times before trying it himself. The first few times, although he managed to catch the sword, he could not complete the movements exactly the same with his right hand.

Before long, he was sweating from the exertion but was able to complete the maneuver.

"Darach, people have gathered in the great hall," Cairn called out from a safe distance. "Ye should come and listen."

"Is Stuart not there?" he responded, annoyed at the man, who'd become overly involved in everything. At the end of the day, he would speak to Stuart and Ewan about Cairn. Something about the man gave him pause.

"He is. However, there are many people here."

Darach stalked over to the man. "I am yer laird. Ye will refer to me as such."

"Of course, my laird, I apologize." Cairn bowed his head. "I am not yet used to it."

"It has been half a year." Darach stalked to the same door he'd exited from and grabbed one of the cloths that hung over a line for when guardsmen walked inside after practice.

After dunking a pot into a rain barrel, he leaned forward and poured the water over his head, repeating the process to rinse off his arms. Then he dried off with the cloth.

He stomped the dirt from his boots and walked inside. The entire time Cairn did not leave his side.

There were people in the great hall, but thankfully not as many as the days prior. He went to the high board and lowered into a chair next to Stuart, who listed to a husband

and wife complain about someone stealing their cows.

Turning to a pair of young men who waited to speak to him, he motioned them closer. "Our da is missing. We think someone may have killed him," the distraught young man explained. "We come to ask for help. We need more people to search."

"Do ye not have neighbors to help ye?" Darach asked astounded that people would not help this family.

The other boy nodded. "Aye, and we have been searching for two days, my laird."

"I will send a group of guardsmen back with ye," Darach motioned for a guard to come close.

"My laird, a word," Cairn said, leaning into his ear.

Darach looked at the man. "What is it?"

"Ye cannot begin the practice of sending guardsmen in search of every drunk husband who decides to spend a day or two away from his home. This is clearly that sort of matter."

Despite him not liking Cairn, the man was right.

He studied the young men for a moment. "Has yer da ever done something like this before?"

Both shook their heads fervently. "No, my laird. Never," one replied. "That is why we are so worried."

The guard waited for instructions with an impassive expression. Darach let out a breath. "Go with four guardsmen and help them search for their father. Just two days."

Next to him, Cairn bristled but remained quiet.

They spent the rest of the morning and well into the afternoon dealing with the people who'd come for hearings. A picture emerged for Darach.

People had not felt heard and had been ignored for so

long, they were hungry not only for food but for leadership.

He spoke to Stuart. "We should plan a festival. Have people come and enjoy a time of celebration."

"That is a grand idea," Stuart replied. "Mother and her group will certainly be excited at the prospect."

"Under no circumstances will a celebration appease the people," Cairn said, with an aghast expression. "To them, it will be yer showing how much better off this family is than theirs."

Stuart leaned forward to look around Darach. "Do ye not have a family to tend to? Ye have spent days on end here."

At the words, Cairn got to his feet and stalked from the room.

"Harsh," Darach said, glad that his brother had found a way for the man to leave. "He has been rather imposing of late."

"I am not sure we should trust him," Stuart replied. "Speaking of not trusting. Where is Gideon?"

Darach searched the room for his youngest brother. "I have not seen him today."

Narrowing his eyes, he considered that perhaps Gideon was keeping an eye on the women. His younger brother had ensured to sit next to Beatrice Macdonald the last two last meals. Was his brother smitten with the lass?

If so, his mother would not be pleased.

"I'm going to find something to eat," Darach announced and stood, stretching his arms above his head. "Then I will find Mother and tell her to plan the festivities."

Stuart took in those that remained in the room and motioned a servant girl forward. "Let cook know to prepare for a midday meal for forty people."

WHEN DARACH ENTERED the kitchen, Greer, the cook, motioned for him to go to the adjoining, small room, where the servants ate. "My laird, what do ye wish to eat?" the woman called out.

"Something simple will do," he replied, sitting and enjoying the solitude of the space while he watched the people in the kitchen scurry here and there. Some kept watch over boiling pots, while others sliced vegetables, and still others set trenchers on trays and began filling them with lamb stew.

Lilia walked over to him with a tray on which a goblet and trencher were perfectly balanced. "Here ye go, my Laird. Ye must keep yer strength up."

The woman leaned closer than necessary to place the items before him. "If there is anything else ye wish, do not hesitate to let me know." Her plump lips pursed, her gaze moving to his mouth.

"Thank ye, Lilia." Darach patted her bottom just as he caught sight of Isobel walking past in the kitchen.

He wasn't sure if she'd seen him touch Lilia. "Go now, I need to be alone," he said to Lilia, who did not hide her disappointment.

Once Lilia left, he began to eat while keeping an eye on the doorway.

Isobel walked past again, this time she hesitated. "May I have a word with ye?" she asked.

"Ye may join me." He motioned to a chair.

Isobel went to a chair that was farther than the one he'd motioned to. "Will yer lady be returning? What I wish to speak to ye about is private."

His lady. So, she had seen.

"Greer," he called out. "Have someone bring Miss Isobel a drink and perhaps some fresh bread."

"There is no need," Isobel said. "They are much too busy."

A cook's helper hurried in, plopped the items before Isobel and rushed back away.

Darach met Isobel's gaze. "What is it ye wish to speak about?"

"My sister."

"What about yer sister? I have barely had time to speak to her. Ye may be aware, I am quite busy and have absolutely no time for frivolity."

"Laird, marriage is not frivolity. Quite the opposite, it is the most serious of matters."

He drank from the goblet studying the woman, who sat back straight, with a most serious expression, and not touching the items before her. From the way she looked at him, she did not care for him in the least.

"Are ye here to dissuade me from marrying yer sister, Miss Isobel?"

Her brows rose just a bit. "I wish to get to know ye better, Laird, and then make up my mind one way or the other."

He couldn't stop the chuckle that erupted.

"Ye have absolutely no say in this matter, Miss Isobel. Ye are but a sister who traveled with yer family. By yer drab appearance, I take it yer parents have a good reason not to offer ye for marriage. I am curious, why is that?"

Her mouth fell open, and she seemed to struggle with what to say. "I did not come to speak to ye about myself. My sister wished me to find out more about ye. Ye see, she is very intimidated by ye…"

"But not by my brother Gideon, who I assume is why I have not seen him all day."

Isobel jumped to her feet. "Sir, ye insult my sister and my family. Beatrice is not with yer brother, but in the sitting room with both our mothers." She rounded the table and pushed a finger into his chest. "How dare ye."

Fury blazed from her green eyes, the anger darkening them until they were almost black. Twisting her lips into an angry sneer, she looked him up and down. "I agree with my sister, ye are a beastly man."

When she whirled around, he took her wrist, ensuring she did not leave.

"I apologize." Darach stood, not releasing her. "Please accept my apologies. I should not have said any of those things."

She looked up at him and Darach realized, that unlike her sister, she was tall coming past his shoulder. "Ye should not have said those things, in that, ye are correct sir, but ye thought them, and that is just as unkind."

Put in his place, he wasn't sure what to say in his own defense. He had been thinking that Gideon was prowling after Beatrice. However, despite his words, he did not consider Isobel unworthy or drab.

"I hold ye in high regard, Isobel. Ye were always kind and I enjoyed the times we visited together when we were young."

She managed to hitch her chin and looked down her nose at him. "That ye are curious about why my parents do not wish to marry me to ye is not yer concern, it is a family matter that will remain private. Ye have no right to know why this decision was made."

Her words only made him more curious.

At his silence, she spoke again. "Now Laird, I find that I cannot speak to ye right now." She snatched her hand from his grasp and hurried away.

CHAPTER SIX

E XPECTING AN EMPTY room, Isobel was surprised to find Beatrice.

"Ye will never marry him, I will not allow it," Isobel exclaimed, storming into the bedchamber she shared with her sister. "Darach Ross has become not only an intolerable brute, but he insulted our family."

Beatrice, who'd been combing her hair in the mirror, turned to her wide-eyed. "What did he say?"

"I will not worry ye with specifics, but enough to say that he is not who ye should marry." Isobel went to her sister. "Why are ye combing yer hair again? Annis styled it nicely this morning."

Beatrice met her gaze in the mirror. "I prefer it down, my head hurts with the tight braid about it."

"It flatters ye to wear it loose," Isobel confirmed, leaning forward to take the brush from her sister's hand. "However, Mother will not like it." She began combing Beatrice's hair, loving the feeling of closeness it brought.

"Is it not silly that we should wear our hair a certain way just because society mandates it?" Beatrice grimace. "Not every style is suitable for every woman."

It was hard to argue with the truth, so Isobel nodded. "What would ye like me to do?"

"Pull it back just at the temples. A simple braid with those strands, the rest I wish to leave unpinned."

Just then the door opened; her mother hurried in with a wide smile. "Honestly girls, it is a beautiful day outdoors, and here ye both are sequestered in the house." She went to the window and pushed the shutters further apart. "I have exciting news."

Instantly Isobel's stomach tumbled, and she closed her eyes. "Mother, I must tell ye something."

"Not now darling," her mother said. "Lady Ross, Ella, and both of ye. Oh, and me, of course, are to be included in something."

The fact their mother dragged out whatever she was to say dramatically, was entertaining most days. However, today Isobel wanted to shake her. "What is it Mother?"

Beatrice sat up straighter with expectation, her hands up ready to clap upon the announcement.

"We are to help plan a huge celebration. A festival." Clasping her hands in front of her chest, Lady Macdonald's bright smile made Isobel grin in return. Despite everything that happened with the annoying laird, a celebration was always a good thing.

Her mother turned in a circle. "We must ensure both of ye look perfect. This may be the day the handsome laird declares his intention to marry…"

"No. He is not a good match for Beatrice," Isobel said, interrupting her mother. "He is not a kind man, in the least."

After a patient sigh, her mother closed the distance between them. "I adore yer sense of devotion to yer sister. Ye would probably find fault with any man that showed interest.

It is time for Beatrice to marry."

Isobel bit her back teeth as she pondered what to tell her mother. That Laird Ross had insinuated Beatrice and Gideon had stolen away. Or perhaps that he'd called her drab. No, that was partially true. Still, he did not have to say it out loud.

"I do not believe he cares for our family."

"Tell her how he insulted us," Beatrice prodded with a stern, but unconvincing expression.

Their mother's eyes widened. "What did he do?"

In that moment, Isobel wasn't sure what to divulge. If she told her mother about his insinuation, she would immediately confront him, and it would turn into an uncomfortable situation since the family bìrlinns would not return to pick them up for weeks. Then there was the personal insult to her appearance.

"He was unkind to me; said I was drab. Then he... well he...should not have said those things to me."

Her mother neared and put her arms around Isobel's shoulders. "Oh, darling. I am so sorry. Yer father and I have often remarked that it will take a special man to understand ye. That ye dress for practicality and care not for fabrics that will only end up torn or stained when ye go on yer treks about the countryside."

Now she felt silly; her mother was right. Her betrothal to a man she'd considered herself madly in love with had ended horribly.

The more he'd tried to mold her into what his family considered to be a proper lady, the more she'd hated it. Too young to know better, she'd tried to please him, even laying with him.

In the end, his family had terminated the betrothal, and

she'd waited months before telling her parents that she was no longer a virgin. By then, her betrothed was married.

If she married, it would be for love and to a man who would not only overlook her lack of fanciful dresses, but also the unseemly fact that she was not a virgin.

"I will be speaking to Mariel," her mother said, referring to Lady Ross. "I changed Darach's nappies and will not stand for him insulting ye."

"Please do not say anything," Isobel said and abruptly changed the subject, hoping to dissuade her mother. "What exactly are the plans for the festival?"

Thankfully, her mother instantly cheered. "It will be held in the field just outside the gates. There will be food, music, and of course dancing. There will be an axe-throwing contest and whatever other unappealing things men like to do."

"Women should be able to compete in things as well," Beatrice chimed in.

"Goodness," her mother said. "I came to fetch ye for mid-day meal. Let us hurry downstairs."

They walked into the great hall. Unlike the days before, today it was only half full of people eating at the tables. The high board was filled as well, with Darach and three of his brothers along with Catriona and his mother.

Isobel kept her gaze away from the laird when she acknowledged Lady Ross and Catriona with a smile. They went to a table where Ella sat and joined her.

"Mother will be anxious that we may discuss the festival without her present," Ella said with a wicked smile. "But I cannot keep from it. There is so much to decide."

They quieted while a servant placed food before them, and

another filled their goblets with ale.

Finally, Beatrice, who looked about to burst, said. "Can there be a competition for women? Why should only the men compete at the festival?"

Ella's eyes went wide. "That would be good. Except, what would we compete at?"

"Archery?" Isobel offered, despite that she wasn't sure how good she was.

"Stoolball," Ella said with conviction. "We will have to wear shorter skirts."

Lady Macdonald shook her head. "Nonsense, I will not have ye running about like milkmaids."

All three younger women laughed. "Mother," Isobel said. "We can change for the game and then put our dressier clothes back on."

Her mother gave her a dubious look and then diverted her attention to the high board, no doubt wishing Lady Ross would come and take her side.

"We can discuss the women's competition another time," Ella said. "Now, we must plan a trip to the village to find items for the festival."

They begin listing what all was needed and despite herself, Isobel began to look forward to the day the festival would begin.

After the meal, the women agreed to meet in the sitting room to work on a tablecloth that would be displayed at the festival. It would cover the table where the visiting lairds would sit. In Isobel's opinion, it was a waste of time. No one would see their hard work since it would be covered with trenchers of food.

She sneaked into her bedchamber, grabbed her sketchbook and chalks, then hurried down the stairs and out the front door. Once outside, she went to a guard, who seemed flustered at her sudden appearance.

"Is it permissible to walk across the field? I wish to go to the wood's edge." She pointed out where she hoped to have good scenery to sketch.

"Aye, ye may. Would ye like escort, Miss Macdonald?"

"No, thank ye. I will stay where the men atop the roof can see me."

Before he could try to talk her out of it, or her mother came out, she hurried through the open gates. Once a short distance away, she let out a breath. Since childhood, Isobel had been unable to remain inside the walls of a home for long before needing to be away.

It was as if she could breathe more freely, and her mind was at ease when taking her walks. She touched the strap of the knapsack that held her art supplies, not ready to sit yet. The field before her was enticingly uneven, patches of tall plants in some areas, while others were covered in low-growing clover. There was a narrow path that ran from the estate, down the incline on which it was built and on through a patch of trees. The path was well worn and must have been cleared for horses and carts traveling through the forest to whatever lay beyond.

Isobel turned away, deciding to go up a steep hill to get a better view of the surroundings. Hitching up her skirts, she began climbing and did not stop until breathless. Then she turned and inhaled the salty air that was as familiar as any part of her body.

From where she stood, she could see a loch and the sea

that spread across the horizon circling the land. In the distance to her left, she caught sight of the small, thatched roofs of cottages on the edge of what had to be the nearest village.

She lowered onto the ground, then pulled her knapsack open. It was hard to decide what she'd sketch. So many beautiful views and so different from back home.

It was a long time before she stopped and studied her drawing. She'd drawn the opposite side, away from the village. It was the portion of land that looked uninhabited, untouched by man. Mountains provided a beautiful background for the sloping hills where sheep grazed lazily in the sun. A lone herder meandered about, his staff in hand as he watched over the flock.

For a long time, she wondered about the man's life. Did he have a family? Where was his home as she could not spot one? Once again, she looked to her sketch and began to add the last few details. Such as the way the sun cast shadows from each animal, showing the way it shined on the side of the hills.

So enthralled in her drawing, she wasn't aware someone was just below until the deep voice called out. Isobel looked down and groaned.

Darach stretched, his hands up over his head. A dark dog ran in circles around him barking and frantically wagging its tail.

When the dog brought a stick to his master, Darach took it and threw it. At once, the animal raced after it.

She could not look away, it was the first time she'd seen him so relaxed.

There was something different about the way he stood there, his arms down by his side as he looked out to the sea,

the wind blowing his golden tresses sideways. He didn't seem
to mind that his shoulder-length hair whipped about his head
as he didn't try to tame it. Instead, he crouched down and
welcomed his dog against his chest when it returned with the
prized stick.

Hugging the animal, the sound of his laughter wafted up to
where she sat, and Isobel smiled at the sound. Even an
unfriendly man like Darach seemed more approachable when
alone outdoors.

Still, she did not care for him. Like Beatrice had said, he'd
changed and was no longer the nice young man she once
knew.

Darach, his dog beside him, raced in a large circle several
times. The dog's happy barks the only sound. He fell to the
ground and again laughed when the dog pounced on him and
began licking his face.

Isobel prayed they'd remain in that position as she hurriedly sketched. It was probably a rare moment for the new
laird to be granted time alone.

From the side door of the home, two men emerged. Both
Ross men. Stuart and Ewan, who were of similar build with
broad shoulders and dark hair, approached their older
brother. The stark difference in coloring between the two who
approached and Darach was striking. And yet, all three had
similar features.

As they began speaking, Darach pulled out a strap and tied
his windblown hair back. He assumed a stiffer demeanor, his
head bent forward as he listed to what his brother said.

A few moments later, the three walked toward the keep.
The dog followed, its stick in its mouth but his tail no longer

wagged.

ONCE THE MEN disappeared into the house, Isobel again studied the surroundings. Soon the sun would disappear behind the trees and the day would end. She made a mental note to come back to the same spot another day at sunset.

For now, it was best she returned inside. Even though her mother and sister were used to her disappearing to spend time alone, the Ross women were not, and she did not wish to come across as rude.

Moments later, in the bedchamber, she put her knapsack away, rinsed her face and hands in the basin, and went to the sitting room.

The women were drinking honeyed mead and discussing the festival. It seemed she'd not missed much.

"There ye are," her mother said with a smile and looked to her hands. "I'd hoped ye would bring yer sketchbook so Lady Ross could see how talented ye are."

Isabel's stomach lurched, and she was thankful to have dropped off her bag. Otherwise, they'd see the sketch of Darach and his dog.

"I only did a bit of sketching today. I promise to do some-thing wonderful and gift it to ye, Lady Ross."

Settling into a chair next to Beatrice, her sister filled her in on what was planned so far for the festivities. She loved seeing her sister so animated and couldn't help but wonder if perhaps Beatrice chose to ignore the fact that she was there to find a husband.

Not only had Beatrice not spent time with Darach, but she acted as if there was nothing to worry about.

"I must apologize for my son," Lady Ross said, looking at Beatrice. "Darach is so busy, he has not made an opportunity to spend time with ye."

At once, Beatrice's countenance changed. With a sharp inhale, she then forced a smile. "I do not mind at all. I am here to spend time with ye and the other members of the family as well."

Lady Ross frowned and exchanged a look with her mother. "Ye are gracious. However, it is time for my son to marry and it would make me so happy if he were to choose ye or Isobel. Yer mother and I have been friends since childhood, we want our families bonded."

At her name being mentioned by Lady Ross, Isobel's mouth fell open. She looked to her mother, but she was smiling and nodding with a warm look to Lady Ross.

Perhaps her mother had not heard the second part of that sentence. "Mother, should we prepare for last meal?" Isobel said, hoping to draw her mother out of the room.

"Not yet darling," her mother said with a dismissive wave. "Tell me, Mariel, why do ye think Darach is so reluctant to marry?"

"I suppose it must be the burden of his duty. Since before the late laird died, Darach has been shouldering the responsibility. My brave son has tried his best to keep our people happy. But it is a monumental task. Ye have been here just a few days and I'm sure ye've noticed how disillusioned our clan is."

Isobel met the woman's gaze. "Perhaps it is not his time to marry. With so many responsibilities, why add another."

"My son will not be forced to marry," Lady Ross said with

a gentle smile. "I wish for all my children to marry for love. However, it is my belief that a love match will ease his burdens, not increase them."

The woman's statement definitely eased Isobel's burden, she smiled widely at Lady Ross. The woman expected for Darach and the others to marry for love. The angry laird definitely did not love Beatrice, as he'd not even tried to make time to spend with her. And even better, he certainly did not love her.

Isobel let out a long breath, her lips curving. "I think we should discuss the rules for stoolball."

"I COULD NOT believe my ears," her mother said when they returned to her bedchamber. She'd insisted Isobel and Beatrice come into her bedchamber and sit so they could discuss what had been said. "Does Mariel really expect that her son will fall in love with someone and in turn said woman will be a beneficial match?"

Beatrice looked to Isobel; her eyes full of questions. "I am not sure what to think. But I am relieved. He is an ogre. I do not wish to marry him."

"Ye have not even tried to get to know him," their mother complained. "Today after last meal, ask him to take ye out to the garden for fresh air."

Her sister looked as if her mother had just suggested she walk with a wild boar, her eyes round and both hands flat on her chest. "I will not."

"For goodness sakes. Fine," she turned to Isobel. "Ye do it."

"I cannot possibly," Isobel replied. "He and I do not care for one another."

When their mother got to her feet and stood in front of them, it was a sign she was very displeased. "Since children, Mariel and I have promised each other not to be separated no matter what our husbands did. Even when our clans battled, we found ways to see one another. The marriage between one of ye and one of her sons will happen. I do not care who or how, but it will happen."

"Mother," Beatrice said in a squeaky voice. "Ye cannot force love."

"I am aware of that," their mother snapped. "Beatrice, ye will go for a walk with Darach tonight. I will see to it." When her mother's narrowed eyes turned to Isobel, it was obvious there was a task for her as well. "I believe Stuart likes to draw. Ask him about it, perhaps do something with him. Sketch him."

Isobel almost laughed at the ridiculous idea that one of them would fall in love and be loved in return in the short weeks they'd be there. But not wishing to upset her mother further, she nodded.

Not giving up, her sister held up her hand as if their mother were a governess. "May I instead speak to Stuart?"

Their mother closed her eyes and sucked in air through her nose.

"Come Beatrice, we must dress for last meal." Isobel grabbed her sister's hand and practically dragged her from the room.

"I do not want to go out in the dark with him." Beatrice's eyes shined with unshed tears. Her sister was truly scared of Darach.

"He is not so bad," Isobel said. "It is not like he will eat ye."

Beatrice's bottom lip trembled.

"Very well, I will ask him to go for a walk after last meal. Meanwhile, ye go find Stuart and go somewhere, so we are both gone and hopefully, Mother will not know who each of us is with."

As they entered their bedchamber, Isobel considered that she herself was a bit scared of Darach Ross.

CHAPTER SEVEN

ARACH SAT BACK in his study, at least free from attending to public duties. There was so much to be done besides seeing to whatever issues people brought when coming to the keep. As important as it was to speak to people directly, there were many other matters just as important that had to be dealt with.

He looked up from a letter he was writing when Ewan and Stuart walked in. After being banished by their father and gone for years, Ewan had returned after the late laird's death. It had been unfair to him, and Darach was sure Ewan would not soon recover from being betrayed by his own father and first wife. Though it had turned out well in the end, Ewan had married a woman that was not only beautiful on the outside but adored his brother dearly.

"Laird," Stuart said by way of greeting. "Ye summoned?" After Stuart performed a low bow, Ewan sat.

Giving Ewan a droll look, Darach motioned for him to stand. "I did not give ye permission to sit."

Ignoring his request, Ewan laughed and shook his head. "How long will ye keep this up, Stuart?"

"Keep what up?" Stuart replied pretending ignorance.

"I need yer advice," Darach began, and his brothers instantly became serious. "There are summons from other lairds asking that I go and to meet with them. A request from the MacNeil to discuss issues pertaining to the Uisdein. And I am also penning a letter to King James to pledge our allegiance. It will hopefully not spur him to ask that I come in person."

He paused and continued. "With the never-ending supplicants, I find myself with no time to do it all."

"Ye need a hand, appoint someone to take yer place in the great hall at least for part of the day," Ewan suggested, and Stuart nodded.

"Cairn is senior councilman," Darach replied. "It would be him who would handle things. However, as of late, I grow more and more suspicious of him."

The brothers exchanged a look and then Stuart nodded. "He has acted strangely. Perhaps nothing to do with us. However, I too have kept an eye on him."

"The farmer who was lost and found injured. He seemed particularly against us seeing to it. When ye decided to send guardsmen to see about him, he insisted on handling it," Ewan said. "I am going to ride out tomorrow to visit the family. If the man is recovered enough, perhaps he saw who tried to kill him."

Although he'd grown more and more distrustful of Cairn, Darach didn't expect it was more than just the fact that the man did not trust his rulings. After all, Cairn had been close to his father. "It would be Duncan's place to serve as my right hand."

Stuart chuckled. "I wish ye luck with convincing him to live here."

"What about Stuart?" Ewan suggested. "He serves with ye daily. If Cairn takes it as a slight, so be it."

Lilia walked in and placed a goblet of wine down for him. "My laird, ye did not attend last meal."

"I have much to do." He picked up the goblet. "Thank ye." While drinking, Lilia circled the table and came to his side. "Ye have had no time for me lately. Would ye care for me to come to ye tonight?"

He considered it for a moment. There was much to do, he expected to work late into the night and would not have time for dalliances. At her delighted smile, Darach hesitated. He took her hand and met her gaze. "Forgive me, but unfortunately I will not have time. I will be working late and will need to sleep."

"Laird, I can take care of ye..." Lilia started but stopped speaking, her gaze moving to the doorway.

"Leave us," his mother said, giving Lilia a narrowed look. "Ye have many other duties to attend to. See that they are done."

Lilia bent her legs and lowered. "Yes, my lady." The woman dared another look to him before dashing through the door. He had to give her credit; she was bold.

"I wish to speak to yer brother," she said and both Ewan and Stuart got up and left.

By the look on his mother's face, she was not at all pleased with him. Too tired to argue at the moment, Darach sat back and waited for the tongue-lashing.

"Ye are not at last meal, and here I find ye with that strumpet. I am embarrassed at yer behavior since our guests arrived."

It became hard to keep his temper in check, but he managed to not bark out his reply. "I am very busy, Mother. I do not have time to sit about and sip mead with yer friends."

Despite himself, his eyes widened when Lady Ross neared. "I know yer duties, Darach. I am aware of the limited amount of time. However, they came with the expectation that ye would marry Beatrice, or at least find if ye are compatible. Ye have yet to spend even a solitary moment with the lass."

"It is ye that demand I marry. I do not see what the urgency is."

"Yer brothers."

"What?" He let out an exasperated breath. "Mother, speak clearly, please. I have things to get back to."

Her face became like stone. "Ye must marry so that yer brothers can as well. Ye being the eldest must set the precedence, ye are aware of that, are ye not? All of ye are well past marrying age."

"Ewan is married…"

"Thank God for it," his mother interrupted. "But ye are a laird."

Marriage and lairdship went hand-in-hand, the people did not trust and respect a man who was not married. It was the way of things and he well knew it. However, despite it all, he had to at least like the person with whom he had to spend the rest of his life with.

"I will try Mother. I apologize." He looked at the spread of parchments, maps, and other unopened correspondence. "I cannot promise much time."

"It is understandable, I know that ye are very busy and do not have time for a full courtship. I do ask that ye do not give the little time ye do have to other…pursuits." She looked to the door when saying the last word, effectively communicating who she spoke of. "I promised the lass that ye would go for a walk with her after last meal."

Darach pushed back from the table and stood. Taking his mother's elbow, he motioned with the other hand. "Shall we Mother?"

Upon entering the great hall, he was relieved that it was empty. He guessed his brothers had something to do with it. They continued through to the family dining room. There were only five people there.

"Lady Macdonald feels unwell and is resting," his mother explained. That left the two Macdonald sisters, Stuart, Ewan, Catriona, and Ella.

"Where is Gideon?" Darach asked. "I have not seen him for several days now."

His mother shook her head. "He's gone to Duncan's to help with something or other. I believe it has to do with a herding dispute."

If anyone could talk disgruntled herders into an agreement it was his youngest brother. Gideon had a golden tongue and a way about him that made people instantly like him. Darach understood why he was summoned to help. It also explained why both Duncan and Caelan, had not come around.

Upon entering, Darach noted Beatrice and Isobel sat at the end, where he normally did. Beatrice to his right and Isobel to his left. The right side of course meant to be where the prominent person sat.

Next to Beatrice was Ewan, his wife on his right. On Isobel's left was Stuart. His mother took her seat at the opposite end and servants rushed in to fill goblets it seemed as if most of them had finished eating.

"I apologize for my lateness," Darach said while looking around the table. "I became lost in my work."

When he looked at Beatrice, the lass seemed to shrink back. It was hard to keep from looking up at the ceiling with annoyance. It was obvious the wee lass found him either intimidating or unlikable. Probably both.

"How fare ye today, Miss Beatrice?" he asked her.

"Well, aye. Well." She gave her sister a pointed look, so he turned to Isobel.

"Have ye found enough to keep ye busy, Miss Isobel?" Darach asked, expecting to get the same reply as her sister's.

Isobel nodded, and her face brightened. "Today I went out to sketch. I too lost track of time, sketching the scenery. Although my reason cannot possibly compare to yers, I understand how it happens."

"What did ye sketch?"

"Well, I did the view of the road that I presume goes toward the village. It is quite lovely, with the forest on one side, the sea on the other."

"Indeed."

He had to admit to enjoying conversations with Isobel Macdonald. Her keen intellect was as interesting as her fiery retorts when she was angry with him.

"Have ye spent time with any of my brothers?" he asked, genuinely curious. Perhaps she'd piqued Stuart's interest. His brother needed to find another woman, as it was obvious his betrothal to the Uisdein lass had been permanently ended.

Isobel considered his reply for a moment and then looked to Ewan. "Yer brother Ewan, his wife Catriona, and I went for a walk by the seashore."

"We did. It was enjoyable," Catriona said.

Darach wondered how Ewan had managed time away for something as leisurely as a walk. As far as he knew, the only time they'd broken from the barrage of visitors was when he'd stormed outside angry, after Cairn had contradicted him in front of a villager.

During his walk outside, he'd not seen anyone walking along the seashore. Then again, he'd been concentrating on playing with Albie, who always managed to alleviate his bad moods.

"Perhaps we can go for a walk after this meal? A bit a fresh air before ye return to work." Isobel's request shocked him. He was fairly sure she did not like him, that she asked him to spend time was interesting. Then he realized, she probably did it to keep him from her sister.

At the other end of the table, his mother bore holes into him. Obviously, she'd heard the request.

"I would like that very much," he replied.

Isobel gave him an incredulous look and he chuckled. The lass was up to something. It could be that once again she would attempt to talk him out of marrying her sister.

"What about ye, Miss Beatrice? Would ye like to join us?"

Beatrice shook her head. "I find that I do not feel well. I hope not to have caught whatever Mother is ailing with."

"Mother has a headache," Isobel said with a droll look. "Ye should come for a walk, the fresh air will solve yer problem as well."

The young lass paled and slid a look in his direction from under her lashes. "Stuart!" she exclaimed, much too loudly. "I am an avid reader, could ye help me find something in yer library?"

His brother turned from a conversation he was having with Ella. "Aye, of course." Stuart grinned and began listing the different selections. Beatrice seemed not at all familiar with anything he mentioned.

"Are ye an avid reader as well, Laird?" Isobel asked him.

"I am, although admittedly, I have not read anything in a long time. I kept very busy helping Father with his ledgers and such." It actually surprised him to note that he missed quiet evenings spent reading.

When the meal ended, he waited for Isobel to gather a wrap, then along with Albie, they walked out the side door of the home to the same place he'd gone to earlier that day.

The dog instantly raced away.

"He will return with a stick," Darach said. "Usually, one that is much too large for him."

Isobel smiled, her gaze following the dog's meandering.

Without preamble, she went to the situation at hand. "My sister has no wish to marry ye, Laird. I must ask that ye consider not courting Beatrice. She is a delicate person, who would be better suited for a quiet life with someone less…"

"Of an ogre?"

"I am sorry for that," she said her cheeks coloring. "It was rude of me."

Darach shrugged. "I deserved it."

When Albie emerged from the woods dragging a branch, Isobel burst into laughter. The sound of it flowing through the air. She pointed at Albie, who wagged his tail vigorously, unable to stop her mirth. "He…he is so funny," she exclaimed between bouts of laughter. "So very adorable."

That she liked the dog more than him bothered Darach. He grabbed the huge branch from Albie, broke off a smaller piece, and threw it. The dog raced off after it.

"Laird?" Isobel began, her gaze lifting to his. "Perhaps ye can inform yer mother that ye will not marry Beatrice. Surely ye do not wish to force marriage upon an unwilling woman."

"Has she not told yer mother?"

Hitching her chin as if in challenge, once again she met his gaze. "Ye know very well that women have little say in who we marry. Besides, she is not yer type at all."

It was too tempting not to tease her a bit. "What, pray tell, is my type Miss Isobel?"

They walked where they stepped down and he held his hand up for her to take. Isobel took his hand not seeming to take much notice. However, the feel of her soft skin, enfolded between his fingers definitely affected him. As soon as she stepped onto flatter ground, he released her hand and clasped his behind his back.

"I would say," Isobel began. "That ye would need a strong woman, who is not intimidated by ye. Someone who yer brothers and yer mother would accept, of course."

"Of course," he said so she'd continue.

"Ye said ye like to read, so yer future wife cannot be a simpleton, but one of keen intelligence. Oh, and one last thing." She gave him a disapproving look. "She must be willing to turn a blind eye to yer dalliances."

In amicable silence, they continued to walk for a bit. Although it meant he would be up much later working, Darach found that he was not in a hurry to return inside.

"What about ye, Miss Macdonald? I know ye do not wish

to speak of why ye are not here for me to court. However, I wonder. What type of man would ye marry?"

For a moment, it was as if she was transported away. She turned from him, her gaze moving from the treetops to the ground. When she spoke, he had to listen carefully, as it was almost like a whisper.

"Above all, he must be kind and forgiving."

It was on the tip of his tongue to ask her what she needed forgiveness for, but intuitively, he knew she'd not speak of it.

"Although often considered a virtue, kindness can sometimes be a fault."

She didn't reply and he ran a few feet away to throw the stick for Albie. When he returned to her, Isobel watched Albie. "Why did ye name him Albie?"

"I was being melodramatic and named him Abyss since he is so dark. However, with a personality like his, it was much too dark a name."

Isobel nodded. "I agree."

"We should head back," Darach said realizing they'd walked quite a distance and it would be dark by the time they returned. He wondered at the oversight of not having a chaperone along. Despite he and Isobel not being at all interested in one another, it could be harmful for her if someone were to say they'd seen them alone after dark.

She turned in a circle, her arms out. "The perfect day is turning into a delightful night. I do love summer evenings."

"It's best we get back before it becomes evening," he replied, looking toward the keep.

With Albie trotting happily in front of them, they began the trek back.

"Will ye speak to my mother?" Isobel asked quietly. "Please consider it."

Darach nodded. "Very well. I am not sure that I have time for a wife. Mother insists on it, however, I'm not sure."

"Ye should marry for love."

The words, so much like his mother's struck a chord. "I do not have time for such things, Miss Macdonald."

"Ye should just call me Isobel. Ye keep switching between Miss Isobel and Miss Macdonald. For goodness sakes, we have known each other since we were children."

"Very well. Then ye call me Darach."

"I cannot do that," she snapped. "Yer a laird."

They reached the slight incline and he turned to assist her up. Just as he did, unfamiliar with the terrain, Isobel tripped and tumbled sideways.

She cried out in pain.

"I will help ye up, do not move." Darach leaned forward and she pushed his hands away.

"I am fine. Just need to catch my breath." She inspected her bleeding elbow. "I feel silly."

Sitting on the ground inspecting her elbow, dark brown waves of hair coming loose from the fall, she was a lovely picture.

"Isobel, let me help ye up." Darach took her arms and pulled her forward. In that moment, Isobel winced realizing something hurt and she pushed forward, perhaps to hop on one leg. All Darach knew was that he lost his balance and landed on his back. Despite releasing Isobel being the smart thing to do, he had not, so she landed on top of him in a tangle of skirts and curses.

CHAPTER EIGHT

I SOBEL GAVE UP her attempts to get up, especially as Darach held her arms. She flopped atop him and lifted her head. "Ye should have warned me."

"Ye fell before I could," he replied dryly with a slight curve to his lips. "Ye should get off of me. Someone could happen upon us."

If she were to be honest, his body was quite comfortable, and she was exhausted from their overly long trek. However, upon catching herself looking at his mouth, she hurriedly stood and held out her hand to help him up.

After sitting up, he looked at her hand and then took it. Once he stood in front of her, he brushed off sand from his legs and bottom.

Taking a cue from him, Isobel did the same.

"Ye will not fool anyone. I saw ye both, cavorting on the ground." The same maid who she'd seen him hit on the arse earlier stood with her arms crossed and a furious expression. With a glare of propriety, she looked from Darach to Isobel. "And ye kind are quick to call us harlots."

She whirled on her heel and ran toward the keep.

"Well that certainly complicates things," Darach said, not looking the least bit worried.

Isobel huffed. "She will not say anything. Especially if it

means our mothers will demand ye marry me."

They began walking toward the keep, in the distance, the maid continued forward, slowing down a bit and constantly looking over her shoulder at them. "She must have spotted us from the upper levels." It occurred to Isobel that the consequences of their being out alone for so long, and then the fall would come to light if anyone else had seen them.

"I would not worry," Darach said and yawned. "I have much work to do. Good night, Isobel."

He hurried away to the same side door they'd entered, the same one the maid had gone into.

"The front door? Or the side door to see what he's about?" Isobel considered out loud just as Beatrice came out the front door.

"Everyone has been looking for ye," her sister exclaimed. "Where did ye and the laird go?"

She let out a breath. "For a walk. We were there within sight for the last while." Isobel pointed in the general direction of where they'd fallen.

Upon Beatrice inspecting her appearance, she added. "I tripped and fell."

"Isobel Macdonald, come inside this instant," her mother stood at the top of the steps with a furious expression. "Ye have given me a great scare. If not for the laird missing as well, I would have demanded guards be sent out to search."

The sun was low on the horizon casting long shadows across the courtyard. Indeed, she had been gone longer than propriety allowed. Considering it was summer and the sun set much later than other seasons, things were definitely going to get complicated unless she came up with a good reason for her lateness."

She limped forward with extra emphasis on her right side and scrunched her face, as if in pain.

"I believe the laird hurried inside to get help. I tripped and hurt my ankle, so we made slow progress forward."

"Oh no!" Both her sister and her mother rushed to her when Isobel moaned.

"It hurts," she said in a high voice. "It really hurts."

With her sister on one side and her mother on the other, they helped her walk into the house. Just as they hobbled inside, Lady Ross and Darach appeared.

Darach gave her a curious look and Lady Ross hurried forward. "Oh, no, dear, what happened?"

"I tripped," Isobel replied, and moaned dramatically when taking a step. "I hope to not have broken my ankle."

"What exactly happened?" her mother asked with an accusatory look at Darach.

"Tell them," Isobel said and noting that no one looked her way, smirked. "Explain why we were so late returning."

With a droll look in her direction, he quickly changed his expression to one of concern. "I stepped up a slight ridge and just as I turned to assist Miss Isobel, she lost her footing and tumbled down like a rag doll."

His mother studied his backside. "Did ye fall as well?" She gave him a pointed look.

"I lost my balance when helping her up, aye," he replied and glared in Isobel's direction.

"That is true. It seems the laird is a bit clumsy."

When their mothers exchanged a secretive look, Isobel's stomach tumbled. They did not believe them. Perhaps her acting had not been convincing enough.

"Unfortunately," Lady Ross said. "I caught a maid accusing the laird of more than just simply falling. In her words, Isobel was atop Darach while they spoke."

Isobel wanted to slap the damn maid. "We were merely discussing how I should get up without harming my ankle further." She crossed her arms in annoyance just as the mouthy maid hurried past and ran outside. It took all her willpower not to run after her and pull every hair out of the wench's head.

"Rumors will not take yer injury into account, unfortunately," her mother said. She then turned to Darach, who'd taken several steps backward, obviously hoping to slip away.

"Ye will marry my daughter."

"Which one?" he asked, looking between Isobel and Beatrice.

"I will not marry him," Isobel retorted. "Ye see how he makes light at a time like this. He has no regard for either of us or our family."

Her mother ignored her outburst and with surprising outrage walked up to Darach and lifted to her toes until almost nose-to-nose with the laird. "I remind ye Laird that I changed yer nappies. I know the kind of man ye have grown to be. A strong and morally just man. Therefore, to keep Isobel from future scandal, I demand ye marry her."

Looking past her mother to her, he regarded her for a long moment with a blank expression. "Very well. Make the arrangements. But it must be after the festival."

"That is a good decision," Lady Ross said with a smile and patted his cheek. "I am delighted."

"We should call on the vicar first thing." Her mother smiled at Lady Ross adding, "There are more things to shop for in the village now."

Lady Ross nodded. "Let us inventory the linens, surrounding lairds and their families will be invited for the wedding of course."

"Of course."

The two women gave her a wide smile and hurried away.

"Isobel? How do ye feel?" Beatrice asked tentatively. "Ye are standing on yer hurt ankle."

Realizing she'd stood steady, Isobel gave up the pretense. "Did ye see that? No one asked my opinion. Whether or not I wish to marry that... that... Ugh!" She stomped her right foot and Beatrice blanched.

"I didn't hurt my ankle," Isobel told her sister as they headed across the great hall. "This is not what was supposed to happen."

"Ye must enjoy his company to have been gone so long," Beatrice, always sweet, pointed out. "That is something."

"Ye do not understand," Isobel said. "Aye, he may be a good one for conversation and such, but he is a rake through and through. Has no care who knows of his dalliances either."

Beatrice's eyes widened. "He told ye that?"

"No," Isobel replied. "I personally saw him pat that maid's bottom, and she was upset and demanding upon rushing up on us just moments ago."

"A rogue without morals. Ye cannot marry him," Beatrice stated firmly. "We must come up with a way for ye to not have to."

There was a foolproof way, but first, she needed to speak to her mother privately. Why did her mother act as if the reason she'd not been offered as a bride in the first place would not be a problem? After all, it was customary for there to be a bedding ceremony, or at least the presentation of the bloodied sheets after a laird's marriage.

Thankfully, many families no longer demanded to be present for the bedding. However, presentation of the sheets was still a popular custom.

No longer a virgin, she would have to find a way to fake the bleeding, however, there was no way to fake lacking a maidenhead.

There were two alternatives as she saw it. Tell Darach the truth and once he rejected her, they'd figure out how to stop the marriage. Or her mother could tell Lady Ross and then they'd cancel the marriage. Either way, they'd have to come up with a way for Darach's concubine to keep her mouth shut.

"What are ye plotting?" Beatrice asked.

"I will need ye to help me tonight. I will speak to Darach and tell him the truth. After, he will surely not wish to marry me."

Beatrice rolled her eyes. "Oh Isobel, that again. Ye are not even sure the act happened. Did ye not tell me yerself, it was quick and painless?"

"We joined. I am sure of it," she whispered. "Neither of us knew what we were doing, but he said he felt my maidenhead."

"Do not speak of that coward. He preferred his hysterical mother over ye. The woman hated ye because ye took his attention away from her. What kind of mother is that?"

Isobel shrugged. "The kind that saved me from a horrible life."

"Yer betrothal was canceled as if it never happened."

Thinking back to the night, Isobel frowned. It had been a hurried affair, both of them nervous and awkward. Her betrothed, Ian, had not bothered to show any kind of affection, but had asked that she spread her legs and he'd pushed inside. At least she thought he did. He'd been quite ineffective if she were to be honest. His member was flaccid and other than dripping sweat on her, he'd not done much more than thrust three times before lying beside her and promptly pretending to sleep.

ISOBEL HAD NO idea what time it was, but the entire keep was silent. Everyone was asleep, except the guards who patrolled the outside. She often wondered what they did to remain awake. One night she went so far as to climb the stairs to the roof of her own home and found some of the men playing a game, while others stood watch. The one she stepped over to gain access to the starry-lit rooftop had been sound asleep.

The men had been shocked at her presence, but soon grew used to her coming up to watch the stars. One man in particular, by the name of Galen, was very knowledgeable about star formations and had taught her to find specific ones.

Now, however, it was a completely different quest that she embarked upon. Without anyone's knowledge, she had to find Darach and tell him the reason why they could not marry. Besides the obvious. They disliked each other. No, that wasn't it. He disliked her. From her perspective, she found him a bit likable, but not someone she could ever fall in love with. He was not the type to be faithful and she would never marry an unfaithful man.

The corridor was dark, and she held up the candle to see better. Heading down to where she assumed was his bed-chamber, Isobel made her way silently in bare feet.

When she came to the door, her heart began to pound. If someone were to find her in the laird's bedchamber, then without a doubt, there would be no way out of the marriage.

Her hand trembled slightly as she reached for the door handle and push it down. The door opened just a bit, and she grabbed the front of her night rail to ensure not to trip. Noiselessly, she slipped into the room and blew out a breath.

The candle gave just enough light that she could make out the edge of the bed. Putting one foot in front of the other, she went to the nearest post, held up the light, and found the bed to be inhabited.

It was not Darach in the bed, but the dog, Albie, who lifted its head and let out a loud yowl. Then upon recognizing her, began wagging its tail and barking happily.

"Shh," Isobel lowered to the bed and began petting the dog with her free hand. "Be silent," she hissed.

The dog rolled onto its back demanding a belly rub and she complied thankful the animal was silent. Hopefully, whoever slept in the bedchamber across the hall would assume it was Darach who'd come to bed as he was most definitely not there.

After a few moments, Isobel backed out of the room. Albie seemed to be satisfied with the attention and curled back into a ball to sleep.

With a long exhale, she reached for the door handle, but

what she touched was definitely not metal.

"What are ye doing in my bedchamber?"

Darach.

Isobel snatched her hand away from what was most definitely not a place any maiden should ever touch on a man. Despite her alarm, she wondered why it had felt much harder than at any time she'd been in bed with Ian.

"I-I... Oh, dear. I cannot breathe." Isobel hurried to a chair and fell back into it. "I do not know why things have become so complicated since coming here."

The laird walked in and closed the door. He was immediately greeted by Albie, who happily barked and whined demanding attention.

"Darach," someone knocked on the door. "Why is Albie barking so much?"

It was Ella.

After a pointed look, he went toward the door.

"No!" Isobel hissed.

But he ignored her, yanked his tunic off, and opened the door just wide enough to look out. "Why are ye up, Ella?"

"I was asleep, but this is twice I've heard Albie. The first time he whined, just making sure he is well."

"He's fine." Darach opened the door wider so that his sister could see the bed. Thankfully, where Isobel sat was not in her line of vision, as the door blocked her.

Upon seeing Darach's sister, Albie jumped from the bed and scurried out of the room.

"Keep him," Darach told Ella and closed the door.

He turned to Isobel and crossed his arms, covering some of the bareness. "Why are ye here?"

"Why are ye half-naked?"

"To convince my sister I was preparing for bed, otherwise, she would have walked in."

"Oh." Isobel could think of nothing else to say.

Darach neared and took the candlestick from her hand. "Explain. I am very tired and need to sleep."

Although she'd spent the last couple of hours practicing her dialog, words evaded her at him being so close. And so undressed.

"Can ye get dressed?"

"What. Do. Ye. Want?"

She gave up on him dressing when he added a log to the fire in the hearth, giving her a full view of his wide back, and leaned his shoulder against the mantel. He faced her and waited.

"I wish to speak to ye about a grave matter. This must stay between us. It has to do with why I cannot marry ye."

He nodded for her to continue.

"If ye are half undressed and we are found out, the worst could happen," Isobel started. In truth, his nakedness was most distracting. For whatever reason, it was hard to catch her breath, and her pulse raced.

"What is worse than having to marry?"

Isobel could have been insulted by the fact, he considered marriage to her horrible, if not for the fact she found it distasteful as well. Since she could not come up with an example of a worse fate, she gave up. "I will tell ye what I have to say and go."

"Go on," Darach prodded.

"Well, ye see." It was harder than she thought to tell someone about her shameful past. "I was…I was… betrothed before. Handfasted actually." The last two words seemed to burst from her and float in the air between them.

"I see."

Isobel got to her feet. "Do ye really, Laird? It is not possible for me to be yer wife. I am not a maiden. Hopefully, yer clan has given up the entire dreadful bedding ceremony custom, but I doubt the bloodied sheet showing will not be demanded by yer… yer… whoever."

The fact he remained still as a statue, his gaze taking her in made her want to scream, which under the circumstance would be most dreadful.

"What will ye do?" It was his turn to take some of the burden of how to handle the situation. In truth, she was growing weary. And also, very sleepy.

"I agreed to marry ye. Given my choices of daughters of neighboring chieftains, I find ye the most acceptable. It is quite doubtful I will grow bored. That is certain."

Her mouth fell open with a retort, but Isobel stopped the first words that came to mind. It would not do to tell her mother that he was utterly mad. He acted as if her not being a maiden was nothing out of the ordinary. "Ye forget the main obstacle."

"Ah yes, yer maidenhead. There is no reason to worry. The sheet will be bloodied."

Her breath caught, and she looked to the region between his legs. "What exactly are ye going to do to me?"

Nearing, his movements like those of a predator, Darach stopped a hairs breath from her. He smelled masculine, outdoorsy, and strangely enticing.

"I am going to kiss ye, Isobel. It is only fair that we do since ye took so many chances coming here."

"I-I did not come to be kissed. I came to ensure ye help me find a way out of this marriage."

"No. I think ye came so that I would kiss ye," he replied with a curve to his lips.

When his mouth came over hers, at first she could not tell what he did. It was as if he was taking his time to persuade her. Then he pursed his lips, the motion so erotic, she could not keep from doing the same in return.

Darach's muscular arms encircled her body and she found herself once again against his chest. This time so very different. Not only because he was without a tunic, but because the warmth of his body permeated through her night rail.

The kiss intensified, his mouth moving against hers, their tongues dancing, their breaths intermingling.

A new world opened for Isobel as she clutched his shoulders, not wanting the sensations to stop. Like the flickering flames of a dying fire once fanned, Isobel's body heated more and more with each passing moment.

Darach's hands traveled down her back and she trembled with anticipation. At the same time, she wrapped her arms around his neck, their kiss becoming almost desperate. Something pressed into her stomach. It was his sex. He'd grown hard and from what she could tell, he would grow even larger still.

"No."

Suddenly, she stood alone swaying in the darkness. Isobel blinked several times and stuck both arms out, unsure if she'd fall sideways.

"I should go," she stuttered and grabbed the candlestick.

Darach had moved to beside the bed, his back turned to hers. "Aye, ye should. I apologize."

"Ye should not," Isobel said. "Please, consider what I said."

When he turned to her, she waved the hand without the candle between them. "This never happened."

With those words, she hurried from the room only then realizing the severity of her scandalous actions.

Of course, Darach Ross thought she'd come wishing to be invited into his bed. She was practically as naked as he was. With only a night rail, she'd not bothered to even wrap a robe around herself.

Once inside her own bedchamber, she hurried to her bed and climbed between the sheets. Thankfully, Beatrice slept soundly in the other bed. Only once she had doused the candle and was swept into utter darkness did Isobel allow herself to breathe.

Her body hummed, sensations she'd never known running up and down her arms, legs, and chest. Of all of them, the heat that pooled between her legs was the most unbearable. Most wonderfully intolerable.

CHAPTER NINE

C AIRN STALKED THE parlor, too angry to do more than ball his fists, he could not utter a single word. The imbeciles had ruined everything.

Someone—he would find out who—had told about their meeting. The laird's guards now patrolled the narrow road to the empty building. He'd had to pretend to stumble upon them and asked what they were doing there.

A guard had informed him that they were on the lookout for a possible insurgency plot.

"Now what?" he growled out loud. "Everything is ruined."

There was a rap on the door, and he called out for whoever it was to enter. A meek woman, who he kept on as maid walked in. "Yer food gets cold, sir. Will ye be eatin' soon?"

Her gaze lifted to his, her attraction to him obvious. If not for the fact he was in a sour mood, perhaps he'd give her what she so desperately needed.

Any kind of attachment, however, could impede his plans. "Aye, leave it. I will eat in a moment. Go on home, Ida."

It seemed for an instant as if she was to say something, but instead, she just nodded and left.

Waiting for her to leave, he returned to pacing. If just one man was caught and revealed it was him who headed the insurgence, he would be hung.

Perhaps, he could seek refuge with Laird Uisdein, the man hated Darach Ross. Upon the late laird's death, the Uisdein had broken the betrothal between his daughter and Stuart Ross.

If he were to go there, it would have to be soon and ensure to have a story planned before any rumors travel. No matter what the circumstance, a traitor was never looked upon with favor, even to a common enemy.

Cairn walked out to his stables and found a young lad that looked after his horses. "I will be riding out. There is food on the table. Eat and wait for me to return. Ye can sleep in the kitchen."

It was but a short while later that he rode from his home toward the keep. His heart sank upon seeing Stuart and several guardsmen riding in the same direction. For a moment, he considered turning around. When he caught up with them, none seemed to find it strange. He pulled his horse alongside Stuart's.

"I go to speak to the laird," Cairn said. "I was not informed of a possible insurrection. I had to find out from a guard."

The laird's brother gave him a bland look. "I do not think my brother has to keep ye informed of his every movement."

"As the senior council member, it would be helpful when people come and ask me questions. It does not give them assurance when I am as uninformed as they are."

Stuart didn't reply, instead looked over his shoulder to the guards that followed. "Make sure ye all eat before retiring. There is no need for any late sword practice."

The men murmured their agreement.

"Where do ye come from?" Cairn asked.

"I visited the farmer who was injured and left for dead. He remains unconscious. I doubt he will live," Stuart said. "We spent the day helping with the livestock and out in the field. Brought food and such for the family."

Cairn shook his head. "A very sad situation indeed. I hope the culprit is found out."

"Doubtful," Stuart replied.

By the time they arrived at the keep, Cairn felt hopeful. They'd not run into any guards being sent to his home, and from what he gathered from Stuart, the farmer would die, and his secret would remain safe.

From that day forward, he'd have to be more careful. The entire reason for his plotting had to be clearer.

He wanted power again. The only way to regain the power he held over the late laird was not through violence, but with intelligence and cunning. Darach Ross, like any other man, had a weakness. All Cairn had to do was find it and exploit it. His first idea of involving others in overthrowing the Ross men was much too ambitious. People were ignorant and too stupid to control properly.

Last meal was being served when he walked into the great hall. Laird Ross split his time between eating with people who remained for the meal and eating with his family in the dining room.

It usually depended on who was there. Since there were visitors for the season, Darach ate in the dining room most days as of late.

Tonight, Cairn was in luck. Not only did the laird eat in the great hall, but he was seated at a table with a well-established local family.

Cairn neared. "May I join ye?"

If the laird was surprised at his late appearance, it was not obvious. He motioned to a chair. "Of course."

Once he greeted the family, he waited to be served while interjecting into the conversation. It was a boring uninteresting dribble about the changes in local customs. Before long, Cairn wished he'd remained at home. There was little he could learn about what happened.

And yet, he had to withstand much to regain what he once had. What he deserved after so many years of loyalty.

The rest of the Ross family emerged from the direction of the dining room and Cairn took notice of the women. One, in particular, the younger of the sisters stood out. She was a beauty that drew everyone's attention.

The laird did not seem immune as he tracked their progress as they went with his mother to stand by the hearth.

"If ye will excuse me," Darach stood and went to the group.

Cairn pretended to listen to the droning of the old man, who continued to spew nonsense about the change in customs, while keeping an eye on the group.

Speaking to the group, probably wishing them a good night's rest, Darach stood next to the younger sister. The conversation continued, the women seeming to ask the laird several questions.

Despite the nearness of the lass, the laird did not touch her, nor did he seem to pay her extra attention.

Cairn blew out a breath. So, the chit would not be a weakness he could explore. Then again, male pride was something that could definitely be used against a man such as Darach

Ross, who prided himself for his masculinity.

The question was how.

As the women walked off, Cairn looked back to his tablemates for a moment. When he looked back to the laird, his lips curved.

The laird leaned forward and whispered something into the older sister's ear. The woman, who upon closer inspection, was indeed striking, shook her head. When she turned and looked to the laird, her cheeks had turned bright pink.

It could be that despite marrying the younger sister, Darach Ross was already grooming the older one to be his lover.

Interesting.

"Excuse me, please," Cairn said, interrupting the man's boring dribble. "I am late to meet someone."

"Laird," he said, nearing Darach. "Would ye mind if I sleep here tonight? It is getting quite late."

After the laird's nod, he pretended to go toward where the guards were but at the last minute hurried up the stairs. At the end of the corridor, he peered around the wall.

The women dispersed, Lady Ross and Miss Ella heading toward their bedchambers, Lady Macdonald bid her daughters good night and walked through a doorway. The sisters entered a bedchamber across the hall from their mother.

Cairn turned back to head down the stairs as a guard walked up.

The young man gave him a quizzical look but said nothing.

"I am looking for an empty room," Cairn said by way of explanation and hurried away.

Down the stairs, across the great hall to the back, was another corridor. The rooms there were smaller and with little or no view of the outdoors.

Lilia appeared just as Cairn turned the corner, and she attempted to hurry past.

He pushed her against the wall and held her in place, both hands on her waist. "Heading to warm the laird's bed?"

"Release me," she said in a low voice.

Cairn pressed his mouth to the side of her neck. "Ye may warm my bed. It has been too long."

"No."

He trailed his mouth from the racing pulse at her throat to cover her mouth. Lilia did not resist.

"Would ye deny me what I've had many times? I know ye enjoy what we do."

Lilia's eyes narrowed. "I said let me go."

"Is he as giving with his body as I am? Do to ye what I know ye like?"

Her breath quickened, but she pushed him away. "Ye can never give me what I want."

"Neither will he," Cairn stepped back. "Once he marries, ye will never darken his doorway."

She huffed. "We will see."

The harlot walked away as if he was nothing more than a nuisance. Instead of going to the chamber that he kept there, he went to a different door.

"THAT DID NOT take long," Cairn said when Lilia returned to her room.

Her eyes widened at seeing him on her bed. Naked on his back, he stroked himself lazily. "Ye need it tonight, do ye not wench?"

Lilia stalked to the corner where she began to undress. With care she removed each item, folding it carefully before placing it over a chair. Her gaze dashed to him and lingered on his hard member. "This means nothing."

"I am aware," Cairn replied, barely able to keep from demanding she come to him. Instead, he looked over her body.

Her curves were enticing. Lilia had large breasts and a small waist that flared out from full hips. Her round ample bottom was his favorite body part. It was a good thing because a man biting and licking her there and in between was one of Lilia's preferred acts.

A long time later, they lay next to each other, not touching. Lilia stared blankly up at the ceiling. "Why are ye here at the keep tonight?"

"I need to take care of some things. Ensure my place with the new laird. Not unlike yerself."

"He is not as easily controlled as his father," Lilia replied. "Ye must gain his trust."

Cairn lifted to his elbow to look at her. "How? He depends heavily on his brothers."

"That is a problem ye have that I do not. Competition."

Unable to keep from it, Cairn let out a bark of laughter. "Ye have not just one, but two women who are in the laird's sights."

Lilia huffed and sat up. "Neither of those pampered chits can compete with what I do for him."

"What if he marries?"

"He will still seek me out, need fulfillment and therefore ensure I am well taken care of."

Cairn doubted it. Despite Lilia's talents, she'd become

much too demanding and assertive. No married man wished that in what should be a discreet affair.

"I would not be so sure," Cairn said with a chuckle.

She rolled her eyes. "Get out of my bedchamber."

CHAPTER TEN

T HE PAPERS IN front of him blurred as Darach attempted to reread the words. He leaned back and let out a breath.

In a chair at the table in the study, Stuart reviewed other documents, entering notes into a ledger. His brother enjoyed keeping track of expenses and such. It suited Darach fine, as he disliked tracking minute matters.

"Lilia is put out that ye turned her away," Stuart said.

Darach looked to the doorway. "She will have to find another lover. When I marry, I will not continue to allow her into my bed."

Stuart studied him for a long moment. "I am sure she will find accommodations elsewhere. However, ye have no way of knowing if the lass ye marry will satisfy ye, or if ye will both enjoy bed sport together."

He'd considered it. From the kiss with Isobel, she'd instantly reacted to him. However, a kiss did not mean they'd be compatible when making love. He considered himself a competent lover. One who liked to try different positions and such, but not too extreme. It was one of the reasons he had begun to tire of Lilia. The woman's appetites ran to a dark extreme that he was not interested in.

"I think it is time for us to seek our beds. Perhaps tomorrow spend more time here than out," Darach announced.

Stuart studied him for a moment. "Aye, and we need to keep an eye on our friend."

"What can he hope to achieve?" Darach asked. "There are too many of us, for him to aspire to gain control."

Stuart shook his head. "The farmer was adamant in that Cairn had gathered men with a plan to distract ye. That is why so many were coming forward with frivolous complaints. I supposed he wishes to make himself invaluable to ye. Gain power that way."

"True. A man who is loyal only to himself is very dangerous. I want to confront him, to crush his throat with my bare hands."

"I understand," Stuart replied. "However, we must first learn who else works with him. Cairn is astute, but he is also a coward. If someone doesn't help him, he loses courage."

As Darach made his way to his bedchamber, he wondered if Isobel would visit him again. He'd enticed her with a promise to speak about their upcoming marriage.

It was a trick since he had no desire to call off the wedding. If anything, after kissing the lass, he was more intrigued than ever to find out what lay beneath her colorless dresses. The night rail had been thinner than her dresses, but the shapeless article had not been flattering in the least.

Darach undressed and climbed into bed, too exhausted to remain awake and wait for her.

SLENDER RAYS OF sunlight from between the window drapes lit on his face and Darach realized he'd slept soundly through the night. Isobel had not come to him, it made him smile to know she had a mind of her own and would not be pressured into something she was not comfortable with.

After a swift knock, Ramey walked in. "Good morning, my laird," the man said, pulling the curtains open.

"Good morning, Ramey," Darach replied and yawned loudly.

Ramey went about the morning routine. He lit a fire in the hearth and then went to the doorway and returned with two pails of water. From one steam rose, the other was cold water.

The hot water was poured into a wide basin, the cold into a pitcher. Then Ramey placed folded cloths next to the pitcher.

Once that was done, he went to the wardrobe, took out a clean tunic and breeches, which he placed on the trunk on the end of the bed.

He returned to the door and brought in Darach's newly brushed boots and placed them at the foot of the trunk.

Darach sat up on the bed and stared into the flickering fire. The flames began to grow stronger as he considered what lay ahead.

"The festival begins at midday, Laird," Ramey said as he poked the fire with a long iron. He slid a hopeful look toward Darach.

"Ye do not have any other duties today. And do not come to see about me in the morning."

Ramey's eyes went wide, his lips curving into a wide grin. "Thank ye, the wife will be glad to know."

Once his valet left, Darach took his time getting out of bed. He was growing lazy, too many days not up until after sunrise.

He washed up and dressed and then went to find a quick meal before ensconcing himself in his study. The quicker he got in there, the more he could accomplish before he was forced out to attend the festivities.

"My laird, what can I serve ye," Greer greeted him as he entered the kitchen. It felt odd for the woman who'd fed him since he was in short pants, to address him as such.

"Just porridge or whatever ye have. I have much to do." He stopped at noting there was an army of cooks in the room who watched him as he walked past to the smaller room and sat at the table.

If anyone was busy this day, it was Greer and yet, she personally brought him a bowl of boiled oats sweetened with honey along with toasted bread and fresh butter. She leaned over and kissed his forehead. "Eat, lad."

"Greer?"

The woman stopped and waited.

"How do ye do so much and still manage to make time to make one person feel important?"

"It is not difficult once ye master time. Every instant that passes, do something that ye must. When ye have free time, do not waste it on something that does not matter. Whether time alone on a walk or working like ye do. Every moment should be used properly."

The woman was so wise, he felt inadequate. That her position was so much lower than his seemed utterly at odds with what should be.

"Thank ye, Greer. One day I will repay ye beyond yer expectations."

The older woman grinned and shook her head. "That I do not doubt."

He ate the food. Although simple, the meal was perfect. Once he washed it down with cold ale, he felt ready to face the day.

"Are ye competing?" Gideon asked when he entered the great hall.

"If I compete in the stone put, Ewan will beat me. If I compete in the caber toss, Duncan will win. In archery, Stuart will." Darach looked to his younger brother smirking and continued, "Perhaps I will do the hammer throw, it could be Gavin Macgregor is not up to the task today."

"I WILL WIN the hammer throw," Gideon said.

"Then I will participate in that one. I can beat ye, I think."

Gideon had filled in recently, becoming more muscular, and was as wily as he was strong. "Ye have not been practicing," he quipped.

Darach blew out a breath and headed to his study. "I have much to do. Sign me up for whatever ye wish. I will win."

"Dance it is," Gideon said with a mischievous chuckle.

STUART, GIDEON, EWAN, and Cairn, along with another member of the council joined Darach in his study. The discussion became somewhat animated after Stuart brought up talks with the Uisdein.

"I believe we should wait," Ewan advised. "The Uisdein is mistrustful of us. Despite sending messengers, he has refused to meet."

Darach looked to the council members. "Surely one of ye knows what happened between him and my father. There must have been an agreement that the Uisdein believes we have broken."

"The Uisdein and yer father were never on very good

terms, as ye are aware," Cairn replied. "The only thing they ever discussed was an alliance based on Stuart marrying his eldest daughter."

Stuart's face turned hard. "And that was broken without any reason given."

"I will try again," Darach said. "Once these festivities and my marriage ceremony are over, I plan to go visit the Uisdein myself."

The men in the room were silent. By his brothers' expressions, they did not agree. The councilmen exchanged looks, but no one contradicted him.

He studied Cairn for a long moment. "Cairn, ye went with my father the last time. If there was something discussed, surely ye were included."

"Yer brother went as well," Cairn quickly said looking to Stuart. "There were no meetings between the lairds that both of us were not present at. I can attest to there being animosity and reluctance on the Uisdein's part. He did not seem to care for the alliance."

"Then why did he agree?" Ewan asked.

Stuart shrugged. "Because the lass and I were intimate."

"Ah." Darach let out a breath. "That makes sense then."

Deciding he would speak to Stuart alone later and find out exactly what transpired, Darach stood. "I must go dress for this festival. Gideon, what am I competing in?"

His brother lifted an eyebrow. "Since ye didna want to lose, I signed ye up for the sword dance."

From the grins and exchange of looks, it was obvious his brothers had planned it together.

"Ye have a challenger. Miles MacTavish is claiming to be a

better dancer and will win against ye."

Darach stared at his brothers. "I will not be dancing."

"It has been announced," Gideon replied. "Ye cannot back out now. Ye will not win the hammer throw, but ye may give Miles MacTavish a good run."

Not sure what else to say, he shook his head and stalked from the room.

DESPITE HIM SENDING the valet off, he was grateful that Ramey was there to help him don his chieftain clothing. Kilt, dark tunic, and a sash pinned with the Ross crest across his chest.

"Sporran?"

"No," Darach replied, annoyed at the thought of the damn thing slapping against him when he walked, or if his brothers had their way, danced.

Outside the sounds of bagpipes and drums sounded and he went to the large windows to look down. Many people had gathered and milled about. A group of young lasses danced, holding hands and prancing in circles.

Blankets were spread and groups of people sat in front of the area, that had been marked off for competitions, and watching the activities.

At the moment, two hogs turned on spits, and he imagined the aroma wafting through the air. It would be a good day for his clan. A day of celebrating, eating, and hopefully the beginning of a tradition.

"Son?" his mother said, and he turned to find her also wearing the clan colors of blue and green. Her hair had been intricately braided into a style that looked like a crown. She'd applied coloring to her face and smiled warmly at him.

"Ye look beautiful," he said, meaning it. "I will be so proud to walk out with ye on my arm."

She blushed prettily. "And ye look stunningly handsome. The women will lose their breath."

Darach laughed. "Will I require guardsmen to keep the hordes of lasses from attacking?"

"That is a good idea."

It had been a long time since he'd felt so lighthearted and Darach couldn't help but hope the rest of the day would continue to feel that way.

They went down the stairs and mounted horses that had been draped in elaborately embroidered caparisons. His brothers as well as Ella and Catriona were already mounted.

Darach assisted his mother to her horse and then went to the large warhorse at the front.

Someone signaled for the drummers to sound the announcement as they made their entrance, much to the delight of the people, who clapped and called out greetings.

They rode in a circle, waving to the gathered crowds. His family threw coins to the children and elderly while some of the people tossed flowers at him.

When they arrived at the stands where they'd watch over the proceedings, they dismounted.

Guards took the horses off as his family went to find their seats. Darach would remain on the ground to greet and wish the first competitors luck.

Four huge men, including his brother, Duncan, lined up to compete in the first event, which would be the caber toss.

"Brother," Darach said, greeting Duncan whose flat gaze met his. If not for knowing his brother his entire life, Darach would say the man was made of stone and had no emotions. But it was not so. His huge brother was a loner, one who could not find a place in the world no matter how hard the family tried to bring him into the fold.

Over the years, they finally came to terms that the experiences that brought him to be distant from everyone was an inner battle that Duncan had to fight alone.

"Laird," Duncan replied. "Ye look well."

"I am glad ye came today." Darach squeezed his brother's shoulder and then continued down the line to greet the other competitors.

Horns signaled the beginning of the games, and Darach made his way back to the stands. Out of the corner of his eye, he caught sight of a cluster of women gathered under a colorful tent. They sat on a blanket with their gowns spread around them, reminding him of a flower garden. It was their hope to attract attention as these women were the type to seek beds to warm that night.

Lilia sat among them, dressed in deep red. Her dark hair pulled up into a pile of waves, some flowing to her shoulders.

At noticing him looking toward her, she pursed her dyed lips and narrowed her eyes. He gave a subtle nod in their direction, and several of them waved back with saucy winks or smiles. Lilia just glared.

Taking one step at a time, he climbed up to where he'd sit. Only once he sat would the games begin.

It felt odd that everyone's attention centered on him, making Darach understand why some men lived for the kind of power that had been laid on his shoulders. He wanted to huff at the idea that many envied someone like him, with the title of laird. In his opinion, the burden of responsibility far outweighed any kind of control or power.

He looked for his mother, as he would sit on her left. His gaze swept past Lady Macdonald, then her daughters, first Beatrice in pale green and then next to her Isobel.

At least he thought it was her. A vision of beauty in a deep amethyst gown that fell just off her shoulders. Around her neck from a velvet ribbon that matched the gown, a circular pendant fell between her breasts, just above the crest.

When she lifted her gaze to him, his stomach fluttered. How could she be so many different things at once?

He hesitated before her and held out his hand. Isobel seemed confused but lifted her right hand to his. Then he kissed the back of it. "Ye will make a perfect wife." Behind her, his brothers cleared their throats, letting him know he should sit so the games could begin. With a wave of his hand, the games began.

Isobel's eyes widened when he settled between her and his mother.

The competition began and he concentrated on Duncan's movements.

"We agreed not to marry," Isobel whispered into his ear.

Darach turned to her. Their faces a breath apart, she was obviously caught off guard as her nostrils flared and lips parted. "Did we?"

He turned back to the competition as it was Duncan's turn. He tossed the caber, the tree flipping and landing a fair margin past the other competitors.

Cheers went up, and his brother held up his arms in victory. His other brothers jumped to their feet and climbed down from the stands to go congratulate Duncan.

"Are ye not joining them?" Isobel asked in disbelief. "He won."

"I cannot show partiality."

Moments later, a victorious Duncan came to stand before where he sat. Darach stood, and his brother bowed.

Darach motioned two young women forward. The lass placed a sash over his shoulder, and a second one pinned a jeweled crest upon it. The crowd cheered when the young women kissed his cheek. The entire time Duncan seemed uncomfortable with the attention.

"Will he not join us?" Isobel asked frowning in the direction Duncan had gone.

"It's doubtful. He is competing again in the stone throw and tug of war, so he will remain with the guardsmen gathered over there." He pointed to where groups of men stood around Duncan.

Duncan removed the crest and handed it to a young lad who raced to the stands. The lad climbed up and held out the item. "Sir said to give to his mother for safekeeping."

Ella took it and handed the lad a coin. The boy grinned widely and hurried away.

Soon they became enthralled with the stone throw. There were three different weights and at the end, each winner came to him and he ensured they were rewarded. Crests and bags of coin were awarded to the men who competed.

"There is an extra crest and bag for the winner in my competition," his mother said.

Darach looked to her. "What competition?"

"Stoolball."

He groaned. "Ye cannot be serious. Who will be playing?"

"All of us," Isobel said.

"In those gowns?" Darach huffed. "This I have to see."

The men's competition took a break as people began to eat while being entertained by dancers who'd been practicing tirelessly and now flashed happy smiles. The dancer's quick footwork was accompanied by clapping along to the appropriate music.

"We must speak," Isobel said.

He took her hand, and her wide eyes flew to his face. "Why are ye so against us marrying? I know yer secret and choose to ignore it. What is the true reason?"

"I have already told ye. Did ye not hear a word I said?"

In that moment, he did not hear very well, his view down the front of her gown took his attention making his heartbeat echo in his ears. The creamy skin enticing him to press a kiss in the most inappropriate places.

"Ye are beautiful when angry, Isobel," he said and then turned away when someone called his name.

Looking up at him, Gideon and Miles MacTavish stood side-by-side, each holding two swords.

"Ye are going to dance, how delightful," his mother exclaimed.

"I-I did not... agree to this." He glared at his brother, who performed an exaggerated bow.

People began clapping the entire crowd looking in his directions.

"I am going to kill my brother," Darach said between clenched teeth.

Isobel watched him with interest. "Ye dance?"

Blowing out a long, annoyed breath, Darach stood, and people began chanting his name. He'd not danced the sword dance since a lad. Even then, he'd only learned it to impress a lass he'd fancied at the time.

He grabbed the swords from Gideon and laid them out on the ground, in a cross pattern. The entire time, his brother hovered over his shoulder. "I have to ensure they are placed properly."

"Their proper place is on both sides of yer neck," Darach replied in a low growl.

When Gideon went to inspect Mile's swords, Darach looked up to the stands. Isobel gave him a bemused look. His mother, on the other hand, smiled widely motioning to him, while saying something to the Macdonald women.

She looked so proud. It wouldn't last. He had no idea what he was about to do.

At the first note, he watched as Miles took a stance. Hands to the sides of his face, fingers up and touching.

He imitated the stance, and when the bagpipes began in full force, it was as if he'd been transported back ten years. His feet seemed to recall each step, turn and jump. At first, the song was methodical but then the tempo picked up.

One of his feet touched a sword and it shifted, Darach did not take time to see if it had moved enough to disqualify him but completed the next few steps as the song ended.

He was winded, sweat forming rivulets down the center of his back. How was it that an actual sword fight did not take as much exertion as a damn dance?

The crowd was ecstatic, claps mixing with shouts and whistles. Despite being annoyed at what he'd been forced to do, Darach had enjoyed it.

He turned to study the swords. Both he and Miles had touched their swords during the dance, but it was obvious his were moved further than his competitor.

When he motioned the two lasses hurried over with a sash and coin purse. He then walked to Miles and held the man's hand up.

The clan approved and began to chant both of their names.

"Thank ye, Laird," Miles said, sounding as breathless as him. "Ye are a worthy opponent."

"I would prefer to beat ye at something akin to the stone toss than fancy footwork," Darach replied with a chuckle.

Miles met his gaze. "I will be competing in archery, next. Ye?"

"Hammer throw."

The men went in separate directions, Miles accepting pats on the back as he walked away to change into something more suitable for archery."

When he returned to the stand, the next competition began. The guardsmen, broken into two teams, competed in tug-a-war.

Soon it was time for his second event and Darach pulled off his sash and handed it to Isobel, who took it. It was a public announcement of their courtship, and it was obvious she knew it by the way her cheeks colored as people began murmuring. He went behind the stands and unwrapped his plaid and then folded it and wrapped again, so it fell just above his knees. Once that was completed, he went to the field to find his place.

The entire time, he wanted to think Isobel watched only him. Like the sun on his back, he sensed her taking him in and being proud. He knew what having a woman's admiration brought. He'd been there on the field plenty of times attempting to impress this lass or that one. However, this time it was different.

He didn't care if he won, although that would hopefully impress her. What he wished for was for her to feel pride while watching him.

Unable to keep from it, he turned toward the stand figuring he'd not be able to see her expression clearly.

Isobel stood out from those around her, the color of her dress bringing out her beauty. Then to his amazement, she held up a handkerchief and waved it. Her gaze directly on him.

In that moment, his chest expanded, and he felt like the strongest man on the field. When his turn came, he turned in a circle and released the hammer with all his might, a roar exploding. From the sounds around him, Darach knew he'd won.

He couldn't keep the wide grin of pride as he held both arms up.

Duncan came up to him and wrapped him in a bear hug. Then his brother lifted him off the ground and turned in a circle. The others joined in the melee, all of them shouting with exuberance.

By the time he went to the stands, he was exhausted, but happy. Since he was the laird, it was his mother's job to give him the prize. However, she prodded Isobel, who made her way to him.

The lasses hurried over and handed her the sash and crest, which she placed over his shoulder. When she lifted to her toes to kiss his jaw, he turned his head and kissed her full on the lips.

Applause and cheers sounded, and in that moment Darach realized this was indeed the best day he'd ever experienced.

The drums signaled the beginning of the next competition, which would be a race between young lads. Darach took Isobel's elbow and they went up to the stands to take their seats.

"Ye are making things so-so complicated," Isobel whispered.

Darach arched a brow. "Or is it ye that complicates things?"

CHAPTER ELEVEN

W HY WAS SHE fighting it so? Isobel had to admit enjoying the day, and even more, the way Darach paid so much attention to her. He ensured she, along with his mother, sister, and her family were attended to. They'd each been fed to within an inch of their lives. Her mother was half asleep, her eyes half-closed, her mouth slack.

Ella kept them informed of who was who, their names and where they were from, whenever the men lined up to compete. Isobel couldn't remember a single name as her entire attention was captured with Darach's movements, how he shifted in his seat, or how he greeted the winners. When he turned to speak to his mother, she wanted to touch his broad back. When he looked to her, it was hard not to stare at his lips or look deeper into his blue-green eyes.

Despite the warmth of the day, a shiver traveled through her when Darach's shoulder brushed hers.

This was ridiculous. How could a man she knew would never be loyal to her, bring so many reactions? There had to be a way to guard her heart, because if she were to be honest, she was beginning to want to marry.

The public pronouncement he made through his attention to her in front of the entire clan was not something that could easily be undone.

She let out a shaky breath.

"Let us go change," Lady Ross stood, her face bright with anticipation.

Darach helped his mother up and then turned to her and the rest of the women to his left. "You realize women have never competed in the games before, Mother."

"From today on when our clan has a festival, they will." Lady Ross gathered her skirts to pass her son. "Come along ladies. We are next."

THE WOMEN'S GAME turned out to be a huge success. The crowds laughed, clapped, and cheered, and at the end of it, Isobel's cheeks hurt from smiling. Several times she'd caught Darach watching her as she hit the ball and then hiked up her skirts to dash around the stool. They'd not bothered to set rules, so men, as expected, stepped in to judge and give them rules along the way.

At the end of the day, she and the others, trudged back to the keep, utterly exhausted. The second day of the festival would be mostly archery and another tug of war, and Isobel looked forward to it.

"I preferred yer other dress," Darach caught up with her. "Although I must admit, it would not have been the best choice for running about like a lad."

Isobel gave him a droll look. "Lasses run too."

"True." He looked relaxed. The hours outdoors that day have given him a golden complexion. "Are ye disappointed that yer team did not win?"

Shaking her head, Isobel chuckled. "Not at all. I expected the kitchen maids would be quicker. Although I must say, I did not know my sister could run so fast."

"Ye and she are very close," he stated.

Isobel nodded. "We are, despite our differences in interests and such."

"Congratulations on yer win," Isobel said, noting his lips curved up just a bit. Throughout the stoolball game, he'd laughed while watching. It could be one of the reasons she'd not won, being distracted by how his face transformed. The man was quite handsome as it was, and when he smiled, deep dimples formed in his cheeks.

Lady Ross, who walked in front of them slowed and weaved her arm through Darach's. "I will sleep well tonight," she announced. "Ye should seek yer bed as well, son. No work for ye tonight."

"Just for a moment or two," Darach said. "Even if I wished to, I suspect once I sit, I may not keep from sleeping."

Once inside the home, Darach pulled Isobel aside. "A word."

Her mother nodded. "I will await ye upstairs," she said pointedly.

His hand on her elbow, Darach guided her to his study. The room was cavernous in her opinion. Dark, until he lit a candle and placed it on a large table that was covered in parchments and other paraphernalia.

"Please sit." Darach's serious expression gave her pause. Whatever this was about, he'd left the relaxed man outside and was now definitely Laird Ross.

Lowering to a leather chair that practically enveloped her, Isobel slid forward to sit on the edge so she could place her feet on the floor. The furniture in the room had obviously been made specifically for the Ross men, who were tall.

"This seems quite serious," Isobel said by way of opening.

He sat in a chair to her right. "I wish to speak about our marriage. There are certain things that must be discussed."

Isobel waited for him to continue.

"I will be traveling to see yer father and make an agreement regarding the alliance of our clans. Although I do not foresee any complications. I wish ye to be aware that if an agreement is not made, we will not marry."

Her chest tightened. Of course, he would not marry unless it was beneficial to his clan. Despite being perfectly aware of the transactions that occurred between lairds, it being stated so plainly made her feel like a bargaining chip.

"Anything else?" Isobel said, not caring to remain in the room. However, she had to make her clan proud and ensure not to tarnish the arrangement.

He shook his head. "The day after tomorrow, ye and I, our mothers, and my brother Stuart will discuss the matter further."

"My father will be in agreement; it was his idea that we come. Although he expected ye would wish to marry Beatrice, that it is I ye picked will not affect his approval. After all, that is what daughters are for. Tools to be used as currency when lairds make alliances and such."

"Ye are not currency."

"Do not say it because ye wish to make me feel a certain way. I assure ye, I am perfectly aware of my lot. As a laird's daughter, I was trained since a wee lass to be a laird's wife."

Darach's face hardened. "My family does not believe in a bedding ceremony and I do not wish to do the presentation of bloodied sheets. Therefore, ye can ease yer mind about that."

It made little sense to her that there would be no proof of the consummation. "How will we prove that we are indeed husband and wife in body?"

"My word that it occurred. I do not lie, Miss Isobel."

For some strange reason, the conversation made her feel differently about Darach. It wasn't that he stated anything that she didn't expect or know. Perhaps it was his tone, every word spoken so plainly, without emotion or warmth.

Whatever romantic fascinations had begun to spring within her that day, were dashed by the conversation. In a way, she was grateful as just thinking about this evening, would assure that she kept her heart protected.

"If there is nothing else, Laird, I would like to seek my bed."

He studied her for a moment. "Ye are upset. I did not wish to ruin yer day. However, it is necessary that ye understand…"

"Ye did not enlighten me to anything I did not already know." Isobel stood and he did as well. She met his gaze, ensuring to keep hers expressionless. "I bid ye a good night."

When he reached for her, she pretended not to notice and walked out of the study. She wanted to run, to race up the stairs and get into bed.

However, she made sure to walk up at a normal speed, even stopping to speak to a maid who wished to share an anecdote about the stool race. Isobel forced a chuckle and told the young woman she enjoyed it as well.

Inside the bedchamber, his mother, her mother, Ella, and Beatrice sat waiting for her. As soon as she entered, her mother motioned for her to join them. "What did he speak about?"

She let out a long sigh. "He wished to inform me that he plans to travel to North Uist to speak to Father. Also, he said that if they do not reach an agreement, he will not marry me."

"Do not worry, lass, he will marry ye," her mother said with a comforting tap to Isobel's shoulder. "What else?"

Her temples throbbed. "That ye, Lady Ross, and he will sit down to talk the day after tomorrow."

Her mother smiled. "Nothing out of the ordinary. Why do ye look so glum?"

Beatrice huffed. "Because she feels sad that he did not declare love or speak of things that lighten a woman's heart. Men are imbeciles."

When her sister neared and wrapped her arms around Isobel's shoulders, it was as if something burst and Isobel began crying. As silly as it was, what Beatrice had stated was true. She'd expected that Darach wished to sneak a dalliance. To kiss her and at least pretend to be attracted to her. Instead, he'd calmly informed her of plans that made it clear, she was nothing but a means to an end. An alliance between lairds.

"Oh dear," his mother said, tugging her hand and kissing it. "It is obvious that my son finds ye fascinating, otherwise why would he pick ye? If ye were but a mere task, he would not have made a choice."

"I just want to sleep," Isobel said, wiping her face and blowing her nose into a cloth Beatrice provided. "It must be the fatigue of the day that has me overly sensitive."

After a few more assurances that in truth made Isobel feel worse, everyone left.

Beatrice on the other hand stormed from the room.

Isobel let out a sigh. Annis walked in looking as tired as she felt, and upon seeing her tear-streaked face, hurried to her.

"Did something happen Miss?"

"My feelings were hurt. That is all," Isobel said. "Do not worry about helping me. I know ye are as tired as I am."

"Nonsense," Annis said and began pulling the pins from Isobel's hair. "Once we get yer hair brushed and braided, ye wash up a bit and get in bed, everything will be so much better."

Annis was right. In her nightgown, she slid between the sheets, and despite wishing to wait to see where Beatrice went, she fell asleep.

AT ISOBEL'S SISTER storming into his study, Darach put down the quill. He let out a sigh. If the lass hoped to seduce him, it was the wrong night.

Her hair had tumbled from its pins, half of it up and some down making her look like a milkmaid who'd just been tupped.

"Miss Beatrice," Darach said but then stopped when she held up her palm and leaned forward her other hand on the table.

"Ye do not deserve my sister. I had heard that Ross men were dark-hearted and without regard for anyone but themselves. But now I know it is true. At least when it comes to ye."

The chair creaked loudly when he leaned back, and he wondered if it needed repair. "If this is because I did not choose ye, do ye not think it petty?"

If possible, she became even more enraged, her eyes bulging. "Are ye really that daft?"

Used to women's hysterics, he changed strategy. "Ye are a beautiful lass, Miss Beatrice."

"Stop talking." She held out both hands now.

"I am glad ye did not choose me. However, it would have been preferable, if ye did not choose my sister either. She is upstairs crying."

Darach frowned. "Why would she be upset? I did not do anything to her."

Her eyes searched his face, and Darach noticed how blue they were. At the moment, however, he was sure they were not normally that dark.

"As laird's daughters, we expected to be married through arrangements. Isobel especially. However, at the same time, we both always dreamed of a love match. That of course is an impossibility."

"What does any of this have to do with her crying?"

"Today was a day when Isobel ensured she looked beautiful. It was the day that ye demonstrated in front of yer clan that she was the one chosen to be their lady. And at the end of her special day, ye sat her down and explained that yer marriage was nothing more than an arrangement. And that ye would not be marrying her if an agreement was not made. Ye thought she'd want to know that she was only worth the price of whatever alliance ye and Father made."

His stomach sank, but he remained silent.

Beatrice was there to defend her sister and the first thing he'd thought was judgmental. Darach wondered if he was more like his father than he wanted to admit.

She shook her head. "I am so very sad for my sister." Without looking at him, she turned and walked out.

He let out a long breath. There had to be something he could do to make things right. Beatrice had been correct in that he'd done something incredibly stupid. The way she explained it made him feel horrible.

At the same time, he'd not said anything she didn't already know. He groaned at his attempt to make himself feel better. Nothing was going to change that he'd been a cad.

"My laird." Lilia appeared at the door. "It is late. Do ye plan to rest?"

"Go away," he snapped. Not bothering to look up.

CHAPTER TWELVE

"WHAT HAPPENED?" CAIRN stalked into Lilia's bedchamber. "I thought ye planned to go to him last night."

Lilia glared at him. "He is not interested in me any longer. I have to find another lover. I cannot return to the measly village." There was a desperation in her that made him itch. The woman had little worth other than her body. A commodity that did not last long.

"Perhaps ye should try a different approach, be softer," Cairn said.

With a calculating gaze, Lilia looked about the room. "I saw it in his face. Heard it in his tone. Darach has already let me go."

"Ye should seduce a dumb sap and get married. Else the laird will send ye away and ye'll find yerself without a sponsor."

"Do not dare to tell me what I should do. I have plans, but first I will ruin any chance at their happiness."

Cairn neared and grabbed her wrists, pulling her up from the bed. "See that ye do and soon. I have it from a credible source that she is not happy with him at the moment. This would be a perfect time."

ALTHOUGH ISOBEL DID not wish to go down for first meal. It would be another long day. A day when she'd have to sit next to Darach all day and play a part. If her cheeks had hurt the day before from laughter, this day there would be no such occurrence.

As she walked out of the end of the corridor, movement caught her attention. A woman came from the direction of Darach's bedchamber and hurried toward her. Isobel turned away, went back to her own room and hesitated at the door.

With her head down, the woman hurried past. It was the same one as always, Lilia.

Obviously, he continued to have her in his bed, no matter that they were betrothed. Needing a moment to calm her emotions, Isobel went back inside the bedchamber and paced.

Blowing out breaths until she felt calm, Isobel went back out.

In the great hall, her mother and sister motioned for her to come sit with them. Just as she sat, Darach appeared and headed down the stairs. When he turned in her direction, Isobel turned to her mother.

"How did ye sleep, Mother?"

"Like the dead," her mother replied. "It was certainly a long day. Another one awaits."

Unlike their mother, who seemed in good spirits, Beatrice scowled down at her food. Her sister huffed. "It will not be as enjoyable today. The only competition is archery, and I can never see clearly where the arrows land when we have to sit so far in the stands."

"There will be music and dancing," their mother said. "That is always my favorite."

After eating, they went back upstairs to prepare for the festival. A beautiful dark blue gown had been set out for Isobel. She recognized it as one of her mother's.

"We'll have to pin it a bit," Annis said. "It is a bit too big for ye."

"I am already dressed," Isobel said motioning to her brown serviceable gown. "I do not wish to spend the day traipsing about in an uncomfortable frock."

Annis slid a look to Beatrice. "Yer mother said ye were to dress nicely today, miss."

Beatrice waved the maid's concerns away. "My sister does not wish to be a prize today."

To her astonishment, Beatrice also refused to change out of her morning dress. "Let us go for some fresh air, sister."

Forgetting for the moment what lay ahead, Isobel grinned widely. "Let me grab my sketching book."

After knocking on their mother's door and telling her they'd meet her at the stands, the sisters hurried down a back stairwell and out the back of the keep. The hilly landscape was easy to traverse in their boots and soon they sat on a rock looking down to where the festival preparations took place.

"I spoke to him last night," Beatrice said looking to see the simple landscape that Isobel sketched. "Told that oaf, how horrible he was."

Isobel shook her head. "For all the good it did. Ye should not have done it."

"It made me feel better to stand up for ye. No one should treat us like that. I will not stand for it."

She nudged her sister's shoulder. "I would do the same for ye. Thank ye for it."

"He seemed to take it in. But he is still a horrible intimidating ogre."

The picture of the woman hurrying down the corridor, a disheveled mess, came to mind. "He has a lover. Will probably continue to have one after we marry. I will speak about it when the families meet tomorrow and demand she be removed from the keep at once."

"Did Father ever have lovers?" Beatrice asked with a pensive expression. "I know Uncle Henry had several, remember Aunt Mairi chasing that one off with a broom?"

Isobel considered it for a moment. "If Father did, he was discreet. I will ask Mother."

"Perhaps it is something all men of wealth do. Have a whore on the side."

"Beatrice!" Isobel exclaimed unable to keep from chuckling. "Please, never use that word in front of Mother."

"That's what they are," Beatrice insisted. "Lying about with men that do not belong to them."

"Men do not belong to anyone," Isobel said. "It is us who belong to them. They remain free, no matter the vows they give during a wedding ceremony. Seems it is the one vow they are not held to."

"Aye," Beatrice replied quietly. "I do not wish to ever marry."

Isobel studied her pretty sister. "Let us pray ye find a man who loves ye and is devoted. There are some. Perhaps one like our own father."

"We should go down in a few moments," Beatrice said, not

moving and taking in the view. "I can see why ye enjoy spending time alone outdoors. As much as I do not care for it, sitting here this morning, I am glad to have done it."

It would be a day filled with possibilities by the view of mountains, the ocean, and colorful displays of the festival. People hurried about, setting up tables, tents, and bonfires, over which flavorful food would be cooked.

A team of maids carrying baskets and buckets crossed the short distance from the keep to the field, to set up items on the tables and water to boiling for the cooking to begin in a short while.

In the distance, a line of carts and wagons traversed the narrow roads towards the festival. Today families would enjoy a rare day of leisure and an abundance of food. The idea of a two-day celebration had been a good one. Isobel could see that it brought the people together and gave them an opportunity to get to know the new laird better.

"We should head down in a bit," Isobel repeated her sister's earlier comment and again neither of them moved. She looked down at her sketch, the landscape she'd drawn had been darkened, the sky ominous.

WHEN SHE CLIMBED the stairs to the stand, Darach was not seated. Her mother's eyes widened at her appearance.

"Ye look like a pauper," her mother said exaggerating. "Did ye even comb yer hair?"

"Beatrice and I went for a walk and lost track of time. We considered it best to be on time than to take time to look like peacocks."

Lady Macdonald looked past her to Beatrice, who sat with

her shoulders back, hands clutched on her lap, looking forward.

"I am not sure it would be a waste of time if ye both hurry and go change. The archery competition is about to start, and everyone's attention will be taken."

On the left side of the field from where Isobel sat, the same tent with the women who'd dressed colorfully again remained. The woman who'd she'd seen earlier stood out, dressed in blue that day. Isobel noted that she looked angry, with narrowed eyes and a pinched expression.

The woman must have felt her watching, because she turned toward the stands, scanning the faces until looking at her. Isobel did not look away, but instead kept her gaze on the woman whose eyes widened slightly before she turned her attention back to the field.

Interesting. Of course, she was aware that once Isobel became the laird's wife, it would be in her power to send her away. It wasn't and would never be in Isobel's power, however, to keep Darach from seeking her out.

Dressed in full regalia, Darach was every bit the laird. He motioned to the competitors and the people clapped and called out their favorite's name.

After a hard elbow jab from her mother, Isobel clapped as well. One of the archers was Stuart Ross. The man every bit a Ross, with dark hair and hazel eyes, stood erect, his stance more of a warrior than an archer.

Most archers she'd seen were lithe and nimble. She had no idea of Stuart's quickness, but he was large and muscular. He kept her attention during the competition, it became obvious that Stuart and Ewan were competing against each other.

Where Stuart was powerful, Ewan seemed to have the edge when it came to agility and trickery. In one event, they had to run to a hay bale, drop to one knee, and shoot. Ewan edged Stuart out easily.

The brothers were so busy in their rivalry, they didn't take note of another archer, one of the keep's guards, closing in on their targets.

Gideon, who sat behind Isobel leaned forward and whispered to her and Beatrice. "Bram will beat them because they are too self-involved. Funny in this situation, but not in battle."

It occurred to Isobel that it was the truth in every aspect of life. One could be so self-involved that they missed out on things occurring around them.

She looked to her mother, who was chatting with Lady Ross. Then she slowly scanned the surroundings. Most people were enjoying the day. Families ate while watching the competition, a group of lasses were gathered in one corner preparing to dance. In the distance, the keep guards kept vigil to ensure everyone was safe.

Men on horseback patrolled the forest edge, while others rode along the roads. There was indeed a lot more going on when one took notice.

The woman Lilia wasn't under the tent anymore. Isobel watched as Lilia looked over her shoulder as she made her way past the stands. She headed in the direction of where the competitors prepared and the armament was kept.

At not seeing Darach, Isobel decided to investigate. If they were so blatant to meet in broad daylight, she would be witness to it.

"I will return shortly," she said to her mother and Beatrice, who was talking with Ella.

Hurrying down the steps, Isobel rounded the stands and then slowed. At first, she didn't see either Darach or the woman. Then she caught sight of the edge of a blue dress.

"She will have me removed. Ye must do something," the woman said to someone who was out of sight. "I will not lose everything because of ye."

"It will be fine. Just remain out of her way. The lass will have other things on her mind than ye." Whoever it was, was not Darach. The voice was familiar, but Isobel could not make it out.

"What are ye going to do?" Lilia asked, her voice shaky. "Do not harm him."

Someone touched Isobel's arm and she jumped. It was Ewan. "My brother is looking for ye,"

She allowed Ewan to guide her back to the front. When she looked over her shoulder, the couple had not emerged from their hiding place.

When approaching Darach, if he did not care for her attire, it wasn't evident. He extended an arm to her and she approached and slipped her hand into the crook.

"Uncle Angus, this is my betrothed, Isobel Macdonald." He motioned to an older man with kind eyes. "Her mother and sister are up in the stands. Ye can meet them after."

Angus Ross bowed his head. "Miss Macdonald, I see my nephew did not exaggerate yer beauty."

"Thank ye," Isobel returned the nod. "Will ye be staying for the day?"

The older man nodded. "Aye, for a sennight actually. My

wife and I came for the wedding."

Isobel was confused. As far as she knew her wedding date had not been set. She gave Darach a questioning look, but not wishing to bring it up in front of his uncle, didn't ask anything.

"I look forward to meeting yer wife."

She looked to Darach. "Would ye walk me back to the stands please?"

"As soon as we hand out the prize to the winner."

Three men from the archery competitions stood side by side in front of the stands. Darach took her elbow and walked with her to where the men stood.

Gideon had been right, Ewan and Stuart won second and third place. Once the prizes were given out, Isobel turned to Darach. "A word."

"Now?"

"Aye, now."

She walked in front of the stands and waved up to her mother and sister with as much of a smile as she could muster. Then once they were out of earshot, she turned to him again.

"I was not informed our wedding date was set."

"My trip to see yer father is only a formality and will take two days. Once I return, we will marry immediately. There is no need to prolong it. Yer mother insisted to mine that we marry before she and yer sister return to North Uist."

A sense of betrayal enveloped her. Why had her mother not said any of this to her? It was to be her wedding after all.

"What about her?" Isobel blurted, looking toward the tent where Lilia was once again. "Will she continue to warm yer bed?"

Darach's face hardened. "No. And she has not since ye

arrived."

The lie made her want to throw up. Isobel let out a breath. "Ye do not have to lie. I saw her this morning. I ask that ye not continue to do it in the same bed I will sleep on."

His eyes narrowed and he looked to where Lilia was. "Very well."

"Must I remain for the rest of the games?"

"Aye, ye must. As my betrothed, it is good for our people to see ye here, with me."

Isobel nodded and turned away to climb the steps back to her seat. Her heart was heavy in her chest. Now she understood why so many women looked so burdened. The fact all control over their life was gone, was weighty indeed.

WITH ALL THE wedding preparations, the days flew by and despite her trepidation of her mother and sister leaving, Isobel did her best to present a happy disposition.

The last thing she wanted was to cause worry to either of them, but her insides churned at noting that not only had the woman not been sent away, but she acted bolder than before, even sitting near the high board for meals.

"According to Laird Ross, yer father was in good spirits during their visit," her mother said while watching Annis brush her hair. "I only wish he could be here for this day."

"Me as well, Mother," Isobel said.

The door opened. Beatrice and Ella, who seemed to have become best of friends, entered. "I have news," Beatrice said. "Ella has invited me to remain here for a bit longer and I think

I will."

Their mother's eyebrows flew up. "Whatever for Beatrice? We have to plan marriage arrangements for ye. It will not be possible if ye are here."

"I could as easily find a husband here," Beatrice quipped. "There are many handsome men about." Her eyes sparkled.

That her sister was not as worried as before about Isobel's marriage to Darach, was because she'd convinced her sister all was well. Keeping the farce going longer could prove to be impossible, especially if she and Darach were not compatible in bed.

"Despite agreeing with Mother," Isobel started. "I do not think ye can choose a husband without Father's approval. We do not have that kind of freedom."

Her mother gave her a sharp look. "Isobel do not be so glum. Ye are about to marry a rather bonnie man, who I am sure will make ye very happy. Yer sister will also have a good match. I will ensure it."

"Beatrice," her mother said. "Ye and I will discuss future plans after the wedding. For now, we must ensure yer sister's grand day goes off splendidly."

THE DAY DID in fact proceed without issue. The ceremony in the family chapel was intimate and lovely.

Despite herself, Isobel wept upon reciting the vows, while looking into Darach's eyes. He wiped her tears with his thumbs as he recited his. To everyone looking on, it was a sweet gesture. Isobel, however, fought to not bat his hands away.

In the great hall, the celebration was attended by only

theirs and a few local families. Since the festival had just been held, the Ross's decided to keep the wedding smaller.

In the following days, Darach and Isobel were to ride into several villages ensuring all were aware of the marriage. It wasn't at all what Isobel envisioned, but it was exactly what she wanted. No fanfare and throngs of strangers there to see her and their laird marry.

Every table in the great hall was filled. Either the families or guardsmen joined in the wedding feast.

Each brother stood and gave a toast to them, poking fun at Darach, who took each barb with good humor.

As the hours passed, Isobel became anxious. The wedding bed loomed, and she couldn't help but visualize Darach without clothing. They would become husband and wife with their bodies; a bond that could not be broken. At least not by her.

He slid a look in her direction. "We should dance."

Taking her hand, he led her to the area that had been left open for dancers and the musicians began a soft ballad. The familiar words of a man yearning for love was sung beautifully by a young man. They circled the room and were joined by several couples.

Isobel felt small in Darach's arms. Her new husband was an accomplished dancer, as she'd learned at the festival. He kept her close as they circled around with the other dancers.

"I will always remember this day Isobel," he whispered. "Ye look beautiful."

Shocked at his words, Isobel looked up at him. There was warmth in his gaze, and she wanted to believe that they'd be happy together. "It is a wonderful night."

When the song ended, he kissed her lightly on the lips, much to the delight of those in attendance who clapped happily.

They returned to the high board just as a group of dancers began performing.

"Ye should go prepare for bed. Ye look quite tired. There is only one thing left and then ye can sleep."

When she met his gaze, he had the audacity to smile.

Something fluttered in her stomach and she met her mother's gaze, who motioned with her head toward the stairs.

When Isobel stood, the room went silent, every set of eyes following her to the stairs. It was then she realized Lilia was not present. To make sure, she looked over her shoulder to where the woman usually sat, and she was not there.

Perhaps Darach had kept his word and sent her away after all.

Her mother and Lady Ross came to her and walked with her up the stairs. No one else would be present when she prepared for bed, as she'd asked that only both mothers be there. It was embarrassing enough having to walk across the room as everyone speculated where exactly she went.

When she walked past the room she'd shared with Beatrice, Isobel blew out a breath. Tonight, her life would change. She was to be the new Lady Ross, taking her mother-in-law's place.

"Will I be sharing his bedchambers after tonight?" Isobel asked, having heard that Lady Ross and the late laird did not share sleeping quarters.

Her mother-in-law smiled. "Aye, Darach had instructed that all yer clothes and such be moved here."

They walked into the large room that housed an oversized masculine bed. The bed was the only furniture Isobel noted. A fire burned in the hearth, and it was obvious that the space was recently swept, the scent of lavender was fresh.

Spread on the bed was a beautiful white nightgown, which she ignored.

Her mother led her to stand in front of a mirror. Annis hurried in and helped her to undress.

Once her hair was brushed out and she sat on the bed in the new nightdress, Annis and Lady Ross went out the door.

Her mother remained and came to the bed. "What happens between a husband and wife is natural darling. Remember to relax and allow him to do what he will. I am sure the laird is experienced in this matter."

Isobel gave her mother a droll look. "I am sure he is."

"Do ye have any questions?"

In truth, she had many. She'd had relations once, with her last betrothed, who seemed pained by the entire experience. For her, it had been swift and confusing. After that one time, he'd not tried to touch her again.

"I suppose it's like two horses when they mate?"

Her mother's eyes widened. "I do not think he will be behind ye." Her cheeks pinkened. "Yer husband will be over ye, he will guide himself to yer center and enter ye that way. Ye should be aware of this Isobel"

Isobel shrugged. "I suppose I am. Mother I assure ye, I can deal with it without embarrassing ye."

Her mother took her hand and patted it. "I wish ye happiness and love. Because if ye love one another, what happens between a husband and wife will be much more pleasurable."

Isobel followed her mother's progress as she walked out. How exactly could love affect relations? What men and women did in bed was something in which only the men found pleasure.

The door opened and Isobel kept her gaze on the ceiling.

"Ye look as if laid out after death," Darach commented, and despite her trepidation of what would come soon, a chuckle escaped.

"I am doing what I was instructed to by our mothers. To lay and wait."

He neared the bed and took her arms pulling her up to sit. "We can talk while I prepare for bed."

"Very well," Isobel replied.

"Did ye enjoy the ceremony today?" he asked, pulling off his boots. "I have to agree with ye, I did prefer the smaller group attending."

Isobel wasn't sure what she'd been expecting, but small talk had not been on her list. "Aye, I did enjoy it. The food was good as well."

"Ye looked beautiful today; however, in this moment, ye take my breath away." Darach removed his plaid, leaving him in only his white tunic that fell just above his knees.

Isobel swallowed against the dryness that developed in her throat when he pulled the tunic up from the hem displaying strong thighs, narrow hips, and a flat rippled stomach.

Her eyes flew to the patch of light hair between his thighs and then just below to his manhood. He didn't seem to mind her perusal and she took advantage, as she wasn't sure to ever see him devoid of clothing again. Not unless he slept in the nude, which she very much doubted.

Darach was magnificently made. His body a depiction of masculinity and strength. At first, she was in so much awe, the idea of joining with him did not come to mind.

However, when his sex responded to her perusal, she realized the growing, hardening member would be shoved into her.

It was definitely going to hurt.

"Take yer clothing off. It is easier to enjoy one another when devoid of all clothes." Darach neared and expertly untied the ribbons at the neckline and then slid her nightgown off.

He climbed on the bed and instead of coming over her, he lay beside her.

"Turn to me wife," he said, and Isobel obeyed.

Their gazes met and she wondered if she looked as terrified as she felt.

"Ye have questions," Darach stated.

Isobel wasn't sure if she did, but she nodded. "I am nervous about how much it will hurt."

His brows came together in a frown. "Ye are not a maid. Did ye not say ye had experienced relations before?"

"Once, aye, but I do not think he was… like ye are."

He took her hand and wrapped her fingers around his staff. "It was the same I assure ye."

"No," Isobel replied, curious as to how soft his skin felt, yet under the surface, he was hard. "I never saw it, I can assure ye, but I know it was not this… thick."

His lips curved. "I promise to make it pleasurable."

"Do not lie to me, sir…" She stopped talking because he pulled her against him and took her mouth. Darach kissed her as if he were starving for her, as if she were a lifeline to a drowning man.

Wrapped in his arms, his hands slid down her back, cupping her bottom and pulling her against his sex.

She released him, placing her arms around him as the kiss intensified. Strangely, within moments, the feeling she'd had once before when kissed by him began to flicker. The longer his lips kept hers captive, the hotter the internal flame became.

Finally, she was gasping, barely able to breathe past the sensations that attacked. Darach released her mouth and licked a trail to her breasts, where he lavished one with attention before moving to the other.

Isobel pulled her legs together as heat pooled between them. She wanted relief but was unsure how it would come.

Lifting his head, Darach placed his mouth next to her ear. "I want to hear yer pleasure," he whispered.

Before she could attempt to understand, he slid one hand between her legs, then he slid a finger into her sex, while at the same time stroking between her netherlips with his thumb.

"Oh!" Isobel tried to push his hand away, unsure if she liked the strange surges that traveled down her legs and up her belly. "What are ye…"

He took her mouth and continued to move his hand between her legs.

Suddenly, she could not withstand it anymore, something was about to happen to her body. Isobel gulped in air doing her best to keep it at bay.

"Relax. Ye will like it," Darach whispered. She bit her bottom lip but then gasped for air.

His mouth took hers and his hand continued the assault until suddenly she broke in two.

Isobel cried out, losing all control.

She clawed at Darach as he positioned himself over her. Unsure of what he'd do next, Isobel prayed he would do something more to quell the flames.

His staff nudged at her entrance and she hungered for it.

"Yes," she murmured. "Please."

With a grunt, he seemed to hold back and then entered her slowly. Much too slow, Isobel thought.

Instinctively she knew it was only with his body that the flames would be doused. At the same time, she trembled with fear. Already, he stretched her, and more was to come.

"I am not sure this will work."

"Shh," Darach said and plunged into her.

A sharp pain tore through her body, and Isobel screamed.

Darach stilled.

"I thought ye said to have made love before," he said with a strained expression.

Tears slipped down her cheeks. "It didn't feel like this." She took a shaky breath.

Darach lifted up a bit, but remained tucked inside her. "Ye were still a maiden, dear wife. Calm down, the pain will not return." He kissed her tear-streaked cheeks and then began kissing her again.

Soon Isobel could not stand him remaining still. "Ye should move or something," she said breathlessly. "I am in need."

Thankfully, he instinctively must have known what her body wanted, because he pulled out and then drove back in again and again.

Each movement had a double effect of soothing and fanning the flames of desire.

Isobel clung to his broad shoulders, unsure what to do other than allow every sensation free reign.

It took all her willpower to keep from crying out, she gasped with each movement that Darach made. His large body took hers completely, while at the same time he did not hurt her in the least.

When she opened her eyes and looked up at him, he was a study in beauty. The tendons of his neck strained as he rocked over her, his skin glistening with perspiration.

Something within her seemed to explode. Isobel grabbed the bedding with all her strength, but it was too late. Everything evaporated until she floated in a night sky, her mouth open in a guttural cry that mingled with Darach's deep moan.

CHAPTER THIRTEEN

WITH HIS SLUMBERING wife in his arms, Darach stared up at the ceiling, unable to move, not wishing to actually. His wedding night had surpassed what he'd expected. Not only was his new wife beautiful, but the lovemaking had been unlike any other time he'd been with a woman.

The unexpected surprise of her maidenhead being intact had been enlightening and made him proud. He was indeed the first man she'd given herself to.

Obviously, her last lover had either been inexperienced or a fool. Either way, he cared not. What mattered was that she was fully his.

It could be that for the first time in his life, he'd allowed himself to remain joined with a woman until finding release. Not only had he felt as if his entire world shattered in that moment, but a strong bond formed within.

Sure, Isobel had no way of knowing how deeply he'd been attracted to her. How he'd wanted to spend every moment with her. Until they'd exchanged vows, a part of him had expected something to prevent their marriage.

She shifted and let out a long breath, the warmth of it fanning across his chest and he kissed the top of her head. It wasn't a comfortable position, his left arm was numb from her weight, but he didn't care to move her away.

The heat of their lovemaking had astounded him. It was evident from her responses to never have been properly made love to. Many times, she'd clung to him as if in fear, while at the same time urging him to continue.

Overcome by emotion, he pulled her against him just a bit tighter. "I vow to never be unfaithful or disloyal to ye. I promise to protect ye and our bairns with my life."

"WE SHOULD DISCUSS the upcoming harvest. The people must be prepared to pay taxes," Cairn said the next morning when the council met. "They must know that ye are not a laird to be cheated."

Stuart turned to the man. "What do ye suggest by way of punishment. The people have very little, most are skin and bones. Whatever was done in the past obviously did nothing more than take what little they had."

The man had the decency to at least look sheepish. He shook his head and regained his usual air of arrogance. "They have little because they are lazy. They do not wish to pay their due."

"Aye, the old trick," Ewan said. "Starving oneself to keep from working."

Cairn's face turned red. "I will not sit here and be taunted. I sat at yer father's right hand because he trusted my council. If ye do not wish to listen to me, then why am I here?"

Darach met the man's gaze. "I give ye deference because of yer years of loyalty to my father. However, as of late, I am learning that my father was not a fair leader, but one who kept my brothers and me at a distance so that we could not intervene in the cruelty of his ways."

"What exactly do ye think happened?" Cairn asked with distaste. "A strong hand is best when leading people."

"But not an unfair one," Darach replied. "I do not agree with yer methods Cairn. And I do not wish for a man, who I do not trust fully, to continue on the council."

Jumping to his feet, Cairn whirled on each of them, his hands curled into fists. "How dare ye? I demand proof of yer accusations. Otherwise, ye must apologize to me."

Stuart motioned to a chair. "Do ye wish to sit and hear what I have to say?"

The man shook his head and remained standing.

"Very well," Stuart began. "The farmer ye stabbed did not die. He told us of the meetings ye held with plans to do harm to our family. His is not the only one whose word I got. We were given names of others there and they told the same story."

"It is because they hate me that those men come against me. I would never do harm to the family to whom I have dedicated most of my life." Cairn inched toward the doorway. "I refuse to remain in the room with ye right now and continue to hear these false accusations."

Guards had been alerted to wait for him to exit. Sounds of a scuffle followed by Cairn cursing them until his voice faded.

Darach had instructed that he be taken to the dungeon.

Just days earlier, he'd ensured that men go down and cleaned the cells. What they'd found had been atrocious. Several dead people his father had imprisoned and forgotten about.

The stench had been so unbearable, the men had been split into shifts to clean it, needing a break to regain their sense of smell.

The slim openings for windows had been widened to allow for fresh air and cots were placed in each cell along with a blanket, a chamber pot, and a stool.

No matter the offense, whoever was to spend time down in the dungeon would not sit in their own filth. One meal a day would be given to Cairn, along with a jug of ale.

Two men had been assigned to be wardens. Both with families to feed and in need of work, they'd happily agreed to take on the job.

"What are ye planning to do with him?" Stuart asked. "Cannot keep him down there for long, it will be annoying to have to remember to go down and threaten him daily."

The others in the room snickered. It was not a humorous matter, but Darach understood the need for it.

"I have someone in the dungeon. I had not considered it when taking over for our father. To be honest, I do not know what to do."

The doorway darkened, their brother Duncan stooped to enter, despite the doorway being tall enough. It was habit, Darach supposed.

His morose brother met his gaze for a moment. "I apologize for my lateness. The man has been taken to the dungeon then?"

"Aye," Darach replied. Strange how having his brother here, who was not even a year younger, lifted a heavy weight from his shoulders.

"Unless ye wish to appear weak before the people, ye will

have to make an example of him. If ye release him, he will go and seek followers to bring more trouble. I doubt Cairn is a man who will accept being cast out."

Darach cleared his throat. "Gideon go see about the guard's training. Stuart, the archers. Ewan, go on patrol with ten men."

Knowing Darach needed time alone with Duncan, the brothers dispersed.

"What happens in the south, and do not tell me all is well. Ye and Caelan have not been free to come here. If it is something I need to send guardsmen for, let me know."

"It is the MacNeil; they are sending patrols often. Our few guards have been approached and questioned. They pretend to be friendly, asking about their duties. However, when putting it all together, it is obvious they are up to something."

Darach sat back. "For whatever reason, the sheepherders started a war with each other. That seems to be taken care of for now. It seems that our father made enemies out of the two clans closest to us."

"Ye must meet with the MacNeil."

"I recently visited the Macdonald. I will travel to visit the Uisdein and the MacNeil. I need ye to come here and take my place brother."

Duncan looked to him for a long moment. "Which will ye visit first?"

"It seems like the Uisdein is the bigger threat at the moment." Darach gave his brother a questioning look. "Will ye take my place while I am gone?"

His brother had been reclusive for a long time. The night they'd caught their father with Ewan's first wife, Duncan had taken Ewan's side. The late laird had secretly thrown Duncan into the dungeon for it. Duncan had been imprisoned before and often suffered night terrors because of it. Their father locking him up was the most horrible of punishments after not having fully recovered from his previous imprisonment. Duncan had remained in the dungeons for a week without food or water, until Darach found out about it and released him one night.

Once free, Duncan had gone to live in the southern portion of the land in their other estate with Caelan. It wasn't until their father died that Duncan returned, and even then, it was only for short visits.

"I know ye do not like being here. I understand…"

"Ye do not," Duncan said. "Stuart would be better suited to take yer place."

Darach huffed. "Duncan, what if something happens to me? Ye are the next in line for lairdship. It is time ye begin to fulfill yer duty to the clan."

The muscle in Duncan's jaw flexed as he tried to control his temper. "If it comes to be, which I pray it never does, I will not take lairdship. I never wish to take the place of a man I detested."

"He is dead. I am not our father. Neither are ye."

It was no use arguing with Duncan. He was as headstrong as a mule.

"Tell me what ye know about the MacNeil," Darach said.

Duncan shook his head. "Not now brother, ye have enough of a burden with Cairn's betrayal. The MacNeil is not an immediate threat. They are at a disadvantage as they have to traverse water to form an attack."

"True," Darach said in agreement.

"When do ye go to see the Uisdein?"

"In thirteen days."

Duncan gave him a confused look. "That is a strange number of days."

"A part of my marriage agreement. That my new wife and I remain near each other for a fortnight."

"Sounds like an intelligent rule. We should adopt it," Duncan said, surprising Darach. "A good way to establish a relationship. Especially in an arranged marriage."

Darach had to agree.

Five days later.

DARACH WENT TO the great hall to find food. It was past the midday meal, which meant he'd been in his study too long. He only stirred because his stomach growled.

He stopped when he saw Isobel sitting at a table with his mother, sister, and her sister. Since he was late to the meal, no one sat the high board. He went to sit next to her.

His mother beamed at him. "I am glad that ye join us for the meal, son."

"It looks as if all of ye are finished," he replied looking to their empty plates.

Isobel met his gaze. "We are enjoying conversation and will keep ye company while ye eat."

The husky undertone of her voice brought an immediate reaction. Something in his stomach fluttered making him feel like an adolescent lad. Darach cleared his throat and motioned for a servant.

While he ate, he listened to them talk about practical matters that he'd not considered. Interesting how the women could be so aware of the people's wants and needs. Things that did not include just food and housing. They spoke of visiting expectant women to ensure the midwives were aware of their upcoming births. The subject of clothing and blankets as well as basic schooling for both lads and lasses in the village was discussed.

Both Isobel and Beatrice spoke of the work they did back at North Uist caring for the elderly and the preparation of baskets with specific items that would ensure they were taken care of during the winter months.

As he listened, it became apparent how much his mother and the women of the keep did for others, while representing him. These works had not been done while his father was laird.

"Mother?" he interrupted.

Her gaze moved to him, lips curving. "Aye."

"All of this that ye've started doing, where are the supplies ye need coming from?"

His mother paled and the other women became silent, their gazes locked to her. "I suppose from here, from yer coffers. I-I should have..."

"Ensure ye leave enough for those that come here to eat and request help. Perhaps some of those baskets can be prepared and stored here for those times," Darach said and continued eating.

He didn't look up as he wanted to allow the women to regain their composure.

When his mother's hand covered his, he gave her a wink. "Ye do good work, Mother, I am very proud of ye."

When her eyes teared up, he wondered if he'd done something wrong. At the first tear slipping down her cheek, he turned to Isobel.

She gave him a warm smile. "Ye should be proud. Lady Mariel has wonderful ideas for great work. We will not have spare time in the least."

The women became animated; Ella appointed herself scribe rushing off to gather paper and quill.

Darach leaned over to Isobel's ear. "Would ye like to go to one of the villages with me tomorrow?"

His wife nodded.

"I best go see what the needs of the people are today." Darach pressed a kiss to Isobel's temple and stood.

There were only a few people there to see him. A couple wishing to marry, several farmers, and a sheepherder.

A family came to stand before him with an elderly couple in tow. "We cannot house them any longer," the woman said giving the elderly couple a side glance. "They are a bother, we have six bairns and no place to keep 'em."

"What do ye suggest I do?" Darach asked, looking to the elderly couple. The man did his best to comfort his wife, who cried into a dirty handkerchief. Their clothing had been mended multiple times, their shoes barely holding together.

The man, at least, looked as if he didn't wish to be there. He looked to the elderly couple with sadness. "My parents do not need much, my laird, a simple cottage."

"We should be the ones to get a cottage," the woman interjected, lifting a chubby bairn higher on her hip.

Darach looked to where Isobel and the women sat. They'd obviously not overheard. He motioned to a servant. "Bring my wife here."

Isobel hurried over, her gaze falling on him, then to the family gathered. "What happens?" she asked standing next to the elderly couple.

"It seems," Darach said. "That instead of honoring his parents, Seac defers to his wife, who wishes them sent away."

The woman's face turned red, and she glared at the couple as if it were them who'd done wrong by her.

"Laird, allow me to explain," Seac said. "I do not want my parents sent off. It is just that we have many mouths to feed and not enough food."

Holding back the urge to point out that he and his wife and the bairns looked quite plump, compared to the thin elderly couple, Darach met the man's gaze until he looked away.

"They should remain here with us for a spell. We can ensure they have a warm roof and food until a proper cottage is built for them," Isobel suggested. By her bright expression, she was anxious to get on with her first project.

"I agree," Darach said, then looked to the son. "If not for yer bairns, I would strip all the farmland and livestock ye have been granted. I would have more respect for ye, if ye'd come to ask for help to build yer parents a proper home of their own. But instead, ye pay heed to yer wife's evil tongue."

The man paled. "I offer my apologies and true alliance to ye."

"Yer land and livestock will be halved. A young family who came seeking a grant will be given the other half. Now be off."

The couple exchanged a look of terrified alarm. When the woman started to speak, the man yanked her back. "Ye have done enough. Let us go."

Already the elderly couple was surrounded by the women and being fed. The woman sat next to Ella, who was showing her some sort of knitting. It was endearing to see them both smiling as they talked.

CHAPTER FOURTEEN

IT WAS LATE when the bed sunk under Darach's weight. Isobel had watched him undress, enjoying the sight of his strong hard body. By the time he neared the bed, he was aroused by her perusal.

For these few precious days, Isobel allowed herself to think that Darach was exclusively hers. She pretended she and her new husband were to be happy together, just the two of them.

When he pulled her against him, while pushing her night-gown from her shoulders, she pressed her lips to his chest trailing her tongue around his right nipple. His sharp intake of breath was enough to encourage her to do more. She nipped at the firm tip and then pressed her mouth to the center of his chest trailing kissed up until reaching the base of his throat.

Darach threw his head back, giving her full access. He moaned when she suckled lightly on the sensitive skin.

Already he prodded at her sex with the hard tip of his manhood, pulling her leg over his hip. Cupping her bottom, he pulled her up to make access easier.

Isobel took his mouth and wrapped her arms around his neck, combing her fingers through his hair.

Lovemaking with Darach had become an addiction. When she wasn't with him it was all she could think of. The lack of control was why she'd thrown herself into projects, in hopes it would distract her from the want.

"I need ye," she murmured into his ear. "I cannot wait." Her core was on fire, smoldering, and liquid.

"Ye have me, wife," Darach replied.

"Darach," Isobel began but then quieted when he pushed her back and drove in with force. Both gasped at the sensation and Isobel could not keep from rocking her hips urging him to move.

Darach pulled out and plunged back in, each time sinking into her body fully. Isobel raked her nails down his back until reaching his bottom. She pressed her palms against each side and pulled him deeper with each thrust.

"Ah!" she cried out nearing her peak, the overwhelming sensations centering at her core.

With deep grunts, Darach began moving faster, his body fluid, each movement graceful and yet purely primal.

Reaching release first, he shuddered while spilling. All went to black and Isobel clung to him as she too lost control.

Darach pulled her onto his chest and pressed a kiss on her brow. Both breathed heavily, his chest lifting and falling quickly under her.

"Are ye fulfilled?" he asked.

She wasn't sure if he meant physically or as his wife. In both cases, at the moment, she was. "Aye, I am. Ye?"

"Very much so. Ye surprise me."

Isobel lifted her head and studied him. Darach was always handsome, however, at the moment relaxed from lovemaking he was breathtakingly gorgeous. There was a flush to his face and his lips were swollen from their kisses. "Why do I surprise ye?"

"Ye surprise me because of yer ardor, yer willingness to allow yer passion free reign with me."

She continued to study him.

He gave her a quizzical look. "What is it?"

"Ye are very handsome," she replied honestly.

Darach chuckled. "Ye say it as if it were yer first time to think it."

"I have thought it before. Today, however, to me ye look more so." Isobel frowned. "I cannot imagine why."

"Hmm," he said noncommittally.

In truth, Isobel had often wondered about why she did not hold back with Darach. Perhaps it was that for now, she trusted him fully. He'd been in bed with her each night, and throughout the day she was aware of where he was at all times.

Things would change soon as each went about their duties, but for the first fortnight of marriage, they were to remain near one another. It was a Macdonald tradition Isobel's parents had demanded and Darach had agreed to. The first few days had passed much too quickly.

"Rest now, we are to ride to the furthest village tomorrow."

She wanted to ask if it was where Lilia was, but Isobel had promised herself not to mention her name to Darach until the time came that she suspected he sought her out. The idea of his body being given to anyone other than her made Isobel want to scream. She pushed the thought away as quickly as it came.

"Ye are thinking," Darach said, his voice groggy. "Sleep."

"I am not sure I can. Beatrice leaves the day after tomorrow. Can we put off going to the village until then? I will need the distraction."

"Ella will be sad. She enjoys yer sister's company," Darach said.

Isobel nodded. "I had hoped she would capture one of yer brother's attention, but so far none show interest. And she doesn't either."

"She's not gotten to know Caelan or Duncan, as neither lives here. Duncan is coming to take my place when I travel to North Uist."

"Who travels with ye?" Isobel's chest tightened. It would be the first time they'd be apart, and she wasn't sure how long he'd be gone.

"Ten guardsmen, perhaps a few more. I cannot bring my brothers as each has duties. We must be prepared in case of attack, if my meeting with the Uisdein doesn't go well."

Isobel sat up. "What if he tries to kill ye?"

"Duncan will take my place as laird," Darach replied as if it were the most obvious thing in the world and what she was worried about.

Blowing out a breath, she smacked his chest. "I do not care about that. What about me? Ye cannot possibly put yer life in danger and leave me a widow so soon."

His lips curved. "Does this mean, ye care for me wife?"

"It is not a laughing matter. I mean it Darach. Ye should bring many more men, or better yet, send a representative."

"This is a matter that has to be resolved between lairds."

"I forbid it." She crossed her arms and fought not to cry. "I will not allow ye to go and put yer life in danger. What is it all about anyway?"

Darach pulled her against his chest. "Things of lairds, Isobel. I have to try to repair the damage my father has done.

Otherwise, there may be war between the clans. As it is, even with my visit, I am not sure there is much to be done to make things right."

Closing her eyes, Isobel held him close. How could it be that she felt as if life would cease without him? Was it love she felt?

"I will not think about it. We will have quite a few more days together."

So much was changing in the next few days. After Beatrice left, she would be alone with her new family.

It wasn't that she didn't feel welcome, and thankfully she'd known them since her childhood. Yet those years she'd not come to visit had been a mistake. She didn't know much about the surrounding villages and Darach's brothers were all so different.

Thankfully, Mariel Ross had visited over the years, and she at least felt comfortable with her. Once the fortnight ended, she'd have to find out her duties and begin a new life as the laird's wife.

It was exciting that the women had agreed to take on projects to help those in need. It would be fulfilling.

When Darach shifted, she lifted up on her elbow and watched him sleep for a moment. The moonlight provided just enough light for her to clearly make out his features. How could it be that so soon after marrying him, such a strong bond had formed?

Already she could not imagine life without her husband by her side. He was so different when alone with her. His demeanor softer, gentler.

Once they did not spend every day together, she'd have to

become used to his absences. Isobel closed her eyes and imagined him going to the woman.

A twinge tightened her chest and she let out a breath. If just the thought of it made her feel physical pain, she couldn't imagine how knowing it really happened would affect her.

She settled against Darach, the warmth of his body enveloping her. A tear trickled down her cheek in the knowledge that in all possibility he'd not remain loyal. If it were to happen, that he sought another, she would never be able to trust him again, nor would she ever be able to lose herself completely during intimacy again.

Knowing it was best to push the thoughts away, she sighed. For the next eight days, she would make the best out of things. Enjoy her husband's attentions and the marriage bed.

Once the days ended, he would travel to visit an enemy laird and he would need her prayers and support. If nothing else, she would send him off knowing she would be waiting.

WHEN MORNING CAME, Isobel woke up to find Darach was already dressing. He stood by the window and peered out. Dressed in tunic and breeches, he forwent wearing a tartan. With the warmth of the season, he preferred to wear cooler clothing.

Isobel slipped from the bed and went to the wardrobe. "Do ye dislike that most of my dresses are so drab?"

When his arms came around her and his lips pressed to her throat, she let out a soft chuckle. "Darach, do ye hate my clothes?"

"I became attracted to ye because of them. I adore yer clothes because it kept others from noticing yer beauty."

She turned in his arms and he kissed her. How she loved the feel of his arms, of his body against hers, and the smell of him. "So ye do think they are ugly then."

The sound of his laugh rumbled, and she gave him a playful swat. "I am going to have new ones made and ye are to pay for them."

"Do as ye wish," he said and then pulled her behind when someone knocked.

Stuart, a guard, and another man entered.

"Apologies," his brother said seeming to have forgotten Darach would not be in the room alone. "I should have announced myself."

"Aye, ye should have. Await me in the corridor," Darach growled. "Go now!"

The men shuffled out.

"It must be something very important," Isobel said to his broad back.

Turning to her, he smiled down. "I am not sure they didn't do it on purpose hoping to get a glimpse of ye."

"That I doubt," Isobel said, enjoying the compliment.

When left alone, Isobel went to the door and cracked it just a bit to hear what the men spoke about.

"He's gone," Stuart said. "Someone came and let him out when Seamus took his leave to relieve himself. Whoever it was must have kept vigil."

"I accept all responsibility and expect to be punished for it," a man said, his voice trembling. "I cannot believe to have failed ye so soon, my laird."

Someone else, probably the guard spoke next. "It has to be someone he paid off. I will begin an inquiry."

"Do it," replied Darach quickly. "Seamus go with him and question every servant and guard who was in the house last night. Ensure each of them gives ye any details of what they may have seen or heard."

After that, the group walked away.

Isobel hurried to dress. If there was a present danger, she had to ensure Beatrice was safe from harm.

After not finding Beatrice in her bedchamber, Isobel scurried down the corridor.

Her hair still down and probably a tussled mess, she stormed into the sitting room where she found Beatrice and Lady Ross drinking tea.

"Goodness, ye look as if ye were dragged behind a cart," Beatrice exclaimed with a snicker. "Is something amiss?"

Isobel shrugged. "I am not sure. Stuart and two men came to fetch Darach. They were talking about someone escaping. I wanted to be sure ye were out of harm's way."

"Ah yes," Lady Mariel said. "Cairn, the traitorous snake. He must have gotten away. I do not believe him to be harmful. His sharpest weapon is that poisonous tongue of his."

"What did he do?" Isobel asked sitting down and began running her fingers through her hair.

"I am not sure. After noting he's been absent, Stuart informed me that he'd be thrown in the dungeon for plotting against our family."

"Goodness," both Beatrice and Isobel stated in unison.

"Let me help ye," Beatrice pulled a small comb from her pocket and began untangling Isobel's hair. "We cannot have ye going down to first meal looking like this. Honestly Isobel, ye must do something about yer clothing."

Lady Mariel laughed. "I will send for a seamstress from the village to come. She is very quick and quite talented."

"Thank ye," Isobel replied. "However, on the days when I plan to go for walks, I will be wearing my serviceable gowns."

Despite herself, she became excited at the thought of new more colorful dresses. Isobel let out a sigh. "Lady Mariel, I find myself growing quite close to Darach. Is it normal? I am fearful of when the fortnight ends and how it will change our relationship."

"I do not think things will change between ye and my son. He is a very loyal man. Believe what he tells ye. Darach is a man of his word. It will be different of course as time passes. He has many duties to see to, and ye will be busy with yer own."

Beatrice hugged Isobel. "It makes me happy that ye've grown close to the terrifying man."

"Do ye still find him so, sister?" Isobel asked with a chuckle.

"Not so much, I suppose. However, I would not care to be left alone with him in a dark corridor." Beatrice shivered melodramatically, making both Lady Mariel and Isobel laugh.

Annis appeared in the doorway, her large eyes pinning her. "Lady Isobel, I've been up and down every stairwell searching for ye. I thought ye disappeared. Heard someone escaped."

This made them giggle harder.

Isobel wiped tears of mirth from her face. "Did ye think I ran away?"

The maid rolled her eyes. "One never knows with ye."

"I am sorry to have worried ye, Annis. I too heard of the escape and hurried to ensure Beatrice was well. Come sit, ye look about to faint."

That Annis was treated equally from time to time did not seem to distress Lady Mariel, who began telling them of her plans for the day. They were to begin the collecting and putting together baskets for the needy.

It was only a bit later that they went down the stairs to first meal. Isobel went to the high board and lowered next to Darach, who looked to her. "Yer hair is different."

Without pins, Beatrice had braided it but left it down her back.

"I will pin it up once the meal ends," Isobel replied, feeling awkward. "I was in a hurry."

"Do not change it. It suits ye, I like it." He nudged her shoulder with his and then turned away to hear what his brother Ewan was saying.

Isobel fought the urge to lean into him. How had she been so fortunate to find such an attentive husband?

"Is everything well? Why did the men come to say someone escaped?" Isobel whispered when Darach turned to his food and began eating.

"Tis nothing ye need to concern yerself with. However, I will have to ask that ye and the women remain here. I might also suggest that Beatrice remain a bit longer. I do not want to spare guardsmen right now to send to North Uist."

Not all bad news, Isobel considered, especially if it meant her sister remaining longer. "I am sure she will not be too disappointed."

After the meal, Isobel and the women gathered in the room by the kitchen to begin the basket preparation. A guardsman came to inform them of what Darach had already told Isobel. Lady Mariel blew out an annoyed breath.

"They best hope I am not the one to find Cairn first. I will box his ears for all these troubles. Now we cannot travel to the village to collect wool to make blankets."

Ella called the guard back, "Who is going to the village? Can they purchase wool for us while there?"

The guard frowned. "I am not sure our laird will allow us to make purchases while searching out a fugitive Miss Ella."

Lady Mariel stalked to the guard, who at this point was becoming nervous. "I will see about this."

"It is one man, who is probably gone far by now," Ella said. "I do not see why all this is necessary." She motioned in circles with her arms.

"It's better to be safe, is what I say," Beatrice exclaimed with a wide smile. "And now I get to stay longer, which makes me glad."

"Me as well." Isobel hugged her sister. "Darach is going away in a few days, and I will be glad for yer company."

Ella eyed them. "Don't forget ye have me as well. And I finally have sisters."

"Aye, of course," Isobel said with a smile. "I am thankful for ye."

Lady Mariel returned. "Darach wishes to see ye, Isobel. He is in his study." She looked to the others. "Lads have been dispatched to the village to fetch wool and other items on our list."

On her way through the great hall, Isobel noted that the elderly couple had set up residence, in a matter of speaking, in front of one of the hearths. They sat in opposite chairs with a table between them. There was a tankard at the man's elbow

and a cup beside the woman. While the man napped content-
ly, the woman mended from a basket on the floor. Her lips
curved as she leaned forward to pet Albie, who lay at her feet
on the floor.

Darach looked up when she entered and stood. He went to
the doorway and closed the door. By his stern expression, she
wasn't sure what to expect.

"I want to travel to the village. I must go to several homes
of prominent families. My brothers are all patrolling different
areas, leaving just one that falls to me to do. Our land is vast
and each of us were assigned a portion upon our father's
death."

Isobel wasn't sure she would agree to them parting ways
before the fortnight ended. "Would ye be gone long?"

He shrugged. "It is about a two hour ride there."

"I will come with ye." Isobel lifted her chin. "I am an accomplished rider. I will not hold ye back."

In the silence that came, Isobel prepared to argue her
point. "Yer mother is of the opinion that Cairn's weapon is his
tongue. She says we should not fear him."

"I do not fear him, but I do not know if he has others convinced to do his bidding." Darach studied her for a moment.
"Very well, ye will come with me."

It was only a few minutes later that they were mounted and
headed for a village north of the keep. They didn't ride at an
overly fast pace. Darach explained that several guardsmen had
already headed there to search, but since there were important
families there, it was best that he be the one to speak to them.

By the time they arrived at the third home, Isobel was
sorry to have insisted on coming. Her bottom was sore, and

her mood was dark.

They were ushered into a large entry and immediately the man, a wealthy merchant guided them to sit and offered refreshments. Isobel was already full, from the last two houses, but etiquette prevailed, and she made sure to eat and praise the food to the merchant's wife who fawned over her.

By the time they left, Isobel was sure her stomach would burst. "How many more stops?" she asked Darach weakly. "I cannot eat another bite."

"We head back now."

A guardsman neared. "She insists on speaking to ye," the man said sliding a look to Isobel.

"Did ye ask about Cairn?"

The guard nodded. "Aye, my laird, and she said to have information but will only speak to ye."

Darach looked to Isobel, and immediately she knew it had to do with Lilia.

"Ye should speak to her," Isobel said with a sinking feeling.

They arrived at a newly built cottage. It was quaint and obviously no expense was spared to ensure every part had been done well. When Lilia opened the door, her gaze went directly to Darach, and then upon seeing Isobel, her eyes widened.

She moved back. "Come inside, please."

Taking her elbow, Darach ushered Isobel inside. The interior was neat as a pin, every item in its place, the faint scent of lavender from dry flowers in a basket wafted through.

"Why could ye not speak to the guard?" Darach said without preamble. "Do ye truly have information?"

Despite Isobel not caring for Lilia, she was surprised by Darach's brashness. Lilia, however, did not seem bothered.

Her lips curved.

"I do have news, but not about Cairn."

Darach frowned. "What is it then?"

"Thought ye should know that I am expecting yer bairn."

The floor shifted under Isobel, but she managed not to sway. Darach on the other hand did not seem as affected. "This is a conversation for another time."

"Another time? Like when?" Lilia snapped. "Ye send me away but ye cannot ignore this."

Isobel was at a loss. A part of her shattered, and as much as she wished to run away, she forced herself to remain still. Would it be proper for her to say something? Was it her place to tell the woman to be quiet and not make demands of her husband?

"I want our bairn to be acknowledged. For ye to claim 'im as yer own."

Darach's jaw flexed, his gaze pinning Lilia. "I am fully aware of many things, Lilia. Tread with care when making demands."

Lilia seemed to lose some bravado for a moment, but then her lips twisted into a snarl. "I have said what I wish. I will go to yer mother, to the clergy…"

"Come, let us go." Darach took Isobel's arm and turned away.

"I hear Cairn betrayed ye. He may know things that ye will not wish to hear. It could be best if ye do not go after him."

When Darach whirled, Isobel gasped at how fast he crossed the room and took Lilia by the shoulders. "What do ye speak of? Tell me, woman. I do not have any patience for yer ramblings."

Lilia had the nerve to laugh. "Yer father confided many things to Cairn. He was there ye know. The night yer mother died. Yer real mother."

Darach shoved Lilia away and returned to Isobel.

They walked out in silence. Isobel rushed around the side of the house and lost the contents of her stomach. Whether what Lilia said was true or not, she sensed something changing between her and Darach.

What if it was true? His first child would be with a lover. Not only that, but the bairn would be born soon after he and Isobel married. Intuition told her, he would be an involved father and therefore would continue to see Lilia frequently.

"I will help ye mount." Darach kept his voice level, but it was obvious he was furious. He motioned to the two guardsmen that waited outside for them. "Stop at the vicar's at the end of town, ask if he saw anything last night."

Isobel wanted to ask for a break, while at the same time, she wanted to be back at the keep. Her heart ached as much as her upset stomach quaked. The temporary escape from reality was over and much too soon, she faced the first hardship of her marriage.

For a while, they rode south, in silence. Finally, Darach spoke. "It is rumored that my father killed my birth mother in order to marry mother. I have always wondered if it is true."

"How old were ye when she died?" Isobel asked.

"Just days, perhaps a sennight, not much more."

The sad story was too much to bear. If it were true, it was something that would not be easy to accept. There was no doubt that Isobel would be heartbroken if it happened to her. "Have ye spoken to Lady Mariel about it?"

"Not in a long time. I will speak to her again. If it did happen, I will not be surprised. What does surprise me is that Cairn would say something to Lilia. She may be lying."

"Does she lie a great deal?" Isobel couldn't bring herself to ask if Lilia may have lied about being with child.

Her husband turned to her, his expression blank. "Do not worry yerself over what she said."

If not for the guardsmen riding so close, she would have erupted at him. Not worry. Was the man daft? Of course, she was going to worry. Not only that, but she had many questions.

It seemed it wasn't only Darach who would be seeking out Lady Mariel. Isobel wanted to cry. Between the rotten end to a long day and the exhaustion, it took all her willpower not to begin sobbing.

And yet, she was glad to have come. Otherwise, she'd never know that the woman claimed to be carrying Darach's child.

CHAPTER FIFTEEN

D ARACH WAS FURIOUS.

Lilia had to be aware he knew she slept with other men and not just him. The only reason she'd divulged being with child—if it were true—was because Isobel was with him. He'd wanted to shake the woman until she told the truth. But he was not one to hurt women.

Not only had she talked about being with child but had brought up the subject of his birth mother's death.

Speculation had been whispered, but never spoken out loud for fear his father would overhear. He was about ten the first time he'd heard the rumor and had asked his mother about it. She'd told him it was lies and he'd believed her. The next time he'd asked, she'd told him that it was something that he should not think about as it did not bring her back.

Over the years, the whispers had ceased. It was only after his father's passing that the rumors restarted. In his experience, rumors always held just enough truth to make the subject a possibility.

Isobel was exhausted. "Do ye want to stop and rest?" he asked.

She shook her head. "Nay. I will rest once we arrive home. I wish for a hot bath and our bed."

Since first meeting her, he'd admired her. Even without

speaking, he saw her inner strength and grace. His wife was beautiful and sensitive.

All that transpired affected her greatly, and Lilia's outburst had hurt her. As much as he wanted to protect her, it was best she find her own way through it. He would be there to provide support and assurance, but in the end, it would be up to Isobel to learn to trust him.

The one thing he knew was that people either trusted ye or they did not. Either way, it came from how one acted and what one did.

"I know this is a hard day for ye." He didn't say anything else as a group of guardsmen rode toward them from the east.

The men remained silent at him sliding a look to Isobel. If the guards had any information, it would wait the hour until they arrived back at the keep.

Soon the keep gates came into view. In a way Darach was glad, for he needed time alone to think. First, he would see to Isobel, she looked about to drop, and he didn't want her to get ill.

They made it through the gates and before she could dismount, he pulled her from the saddle and carried her to the house.

"I can walk," she protested weakly. "Ye do not have to carry me. I am sure ye are tired as well."

"I am used to long rides, ye are not. I should have brought a carriage."

Upon entering they were greeted by his mother. "Goodness, is something wrong?" Her gaze moved from his face to Isobel's.

Darach shook his head. "Nay, the day was too long for her.

My wife requires a hot bath and a meal, and then she must go to bed."

Annis, the woman who came as a companion to Isobel, came close and upon hearing him, rushed away to do as he instructed.

"Honestly, Darach, I am fine," Isobel said, her cheeks pinkening when Ella and Beatrice appeared in the corridor outside their bedchamber. "Ye can put me down."

"Allow yer husband to do it," Beatrice called out. "I find it romantic."

Darach could not help but feel chivalrous at the words.

Once inside their bedchamber, he helped her undress and wrapped her in her robe as maids came in with a wooden tub and pails of water. Soon she sunk into the tub and let out a sigh.

Not wishing to be away from her, but with much to do, he left her to Annis.

"What happened?" his mother said when he reached the bottom of the stairs. "Isobel looks not only exhausted but also upset."

"She is." He took her elbow and ushered her to his study. "Await me here, I must speak to guardsmen. I will not be long."

In the courtyard, another set of patrols that included his brothers had arrived. When a guard approached, Darach instructed the man to wait for his brothers and then wait for him in the great hall, before discussing any findings.

Once in his study, he went directly to the sideboard and poured a glass of whiskey. "I must say, this was an exhausting day. If it were not for that damn fortnight rule, I would have insisted Isobel remain here."

"It is a good rule and ye should have sent someone in yer stead," his mother replied. "What happened?"

He considered which subject to broach first. Finally, he met his mother's eyes thankful, for how she'd never wavered in her love and devotion to him. "Lilia informed me, in front of Isobel, that she is expecting a bairn. Claims it to be mine."

"Poor Isobel. I cannot imagine hearing such a thing so soon after marrying," his mother replied, not seeming shocked.

She let out a breath and pinned him with a stern look. Do ye think it is yers? We all know she warmed more than just yer bed."

"I cannot be convinced it is. I think she said it to shock Isobel."

"I am sure it worked. She looked to be in shock."

Darach clenched his jaw. "No sooner had we walk outside, did she become sick."

"I will speak to a midwife and have her call upon Lilia. This has to be dealt with swiftly. Yer first bairn will not be a bastard."

When she stood, Darach spoke, "She said Cairn was present when my birth mother died. Said something about the rumors surrounding her death and said to ask ye about it."

"That venomous snake. I should have insisted she be tossed out long ago. Ye and the others were blinded by what she gave and did not pay attention to her horrible manner."

"I must ask Mother…"

His mother shook her head. "I heard the same things. That yer father killed yer mother. Smothered her to death while she recovered from yer birth. I tried to ask the servants, but none would talk. They were terrified of yer father. I will find the midwife, I believe she still lives in the village near Duncan and Caelan. Back then, she assured me yer mother died from losing too much blood, but I will question her again. And I will get the truth from her. For now, ye care for current matters. I will find out what I can about yer mother."

"Ye are my mother as well, and I will never see ye as anything else," Darach said, coming to her. "But I must know."

When she cupped his face, Darach kissed her brow. "Do not worry son. Go on and take care of all that ye must."

He walked out to speak to the guardsmen who'd gathered and found that no one heard or saw anything about Cairn. It was as if the man had vanished into thin air.

"I do not think he will cause any more problems," Stuart said. "He is probably traveling far, fearful at being caught and put to his death."

The others agreed, and like him his brothers were angry that the man got away. "We must find out who let him out," Darach said, looking around the room. "Someone must have seen something."

One of the men in the room motioned to speak, and Darach nodded in his direction. "A pair of us saw a man walking toward the woods last night. We called out, but he was too far to hear us. A patrol was sent after him. They found a hunter who claimed not to have seen anyone else about. That was all."

After more discussion, everyone was dismissed. A pair of patrols had been dispatched to the northern and southern shores to search for Cairn. Hopefully, they'd arrive in time to stop the traitor from hiring a birlinn and escaping to a faraway destination.

He couldn't be still, most of the people who'd stayed for the day were heading home, so he walked over to a couple from a nearby farm and wished them well.

"Darach," Ewan crossed from the stables to him. "I believe the person who allowed Cairn to escape was one of our guardsmen. What worries me is whether the man did it for coin or because he is loyal to him."

"Probably coin," Darach replied and yawned. "I will bathe and seek my bed. It has been a long tiresome day."

"Did something else happen?" His brother studied him. "Ye seem worried."

Darach told Ewan about the interaction with Lilia and how it had affected Isobel while Ewan listened quietly.

"Lilia is probably lying. If she is not, who the bairn's father is will not be easy to prove."

"Aye, I am aware," Darach replied. "What worries me is Isobel. Lilia, I can deal with."

For a moment, he thought Ewan wouldn't say anything, but his brother placed a hand on his shoulder. "Ye must reassure yer wife. The idea of yer first bairn coming from another woman is not something most wives can easily forgive."

"It happened before..."

"It matters not."

Darach raked his fingers through his tangled hair. "I have to travel in a few days. I hope to have this matter resolved by then. Mother is sending a midwife to examine Lilia."

"Good."

AFTER MAKING USE of the bathing room near the guard's quarters, he trudged up the stairs to seek his bed. The bedchamber was silent. Except for a single candle, there was no other light. The fire in the hearth had waned so he added a log to it.

Once that was done, he removed his clothing and climbed into bed.

Unlike most nights, Isobel slept on her side with her back toward him. A firm message that she was not happy with him. He considered pulling her into his arms but decided against it. He would give her time to calm down before pushing her.

Despite the exhaustion, Darach could not sleep. If Cairn went to the Uisdein, he could share many things about the clan that the laird would be able to use against them. There was a chance that despite the rift between the clans, the laird would give Cairn harbor, in hope of learning information.

It was imperative that he travel soon and come to some sort of agreement to keep his clan from harm.

WHEN ISOBEL AWAKENED, Darach was already dressed. He neared the bed and kissed her. "How do ye feel? Sore from all the riding?"

She sighed. "Not too much."

"Ye could remain here and rest. I can send someone with food."

"Nonsense," she said, sitting up. "I am perfectly able to go downstairs. There is much to be done and I do not plan to spend the day dawdling about."

By the way she slipped out of bed and crossed the room, he didn't notice any limp or stiffness.

Darach went to her and pulled her into his arms, kissing her brow.

"I have much to do," Isobel pulled away and went to the wardrobe. She kept her face turned away from him as she sorted through the clothes.

"Isobel?" Darach began and stopped, not sure exactly what to say.

"Hmm?"

"I am going to first meal. After I have to meet with several people to discuss who will be taking Cairn's place."

She nodded without speaking.

Walking closer, he pulled her arm turning her to him. "Isobel when I vowed to be forever faithful and loyal to ye, I meant it. Ye never have to question it. Do not ever feel as if ye cannot come to me and question what I do and where I am at all times."

"I am not sure I'm able to discuss this right now. What burdens me..." Isobel sniffed and tried to turn away, but Darach pulled her closer.

She leaned wearily against his chest. "If that bairn is yers, yer first child will be with her."

"I doubt it is mine. I never...finished inside her."

Her eyes lifted to his, they were hopeful and wary. "Can ye do that?"

Her innocence was endearing. "Aye, I can. Although not a certainty, it is a good way to keep from unwanted consequences."

When she let out a sigh and leaned against his chest, it was as if a burden lifted from his shoulders. "Thank God. I do hope it worked then."

"As do I. Mother is sending a midwife to see about what Lilia claims. I have not laid with her since before ye came to visit…"

"I saw her coming from yer bedchamber, just before the festival." Isobel looked up at him. "She was in her night-clothes."

He shook his head. "She may have been skulking about. Trying to spy on us. I do not know why else she would be about."

THE DAYS PASSED swiftly and soon it came time for Darach to depart and head north to meet with the Uisdein. Although not a reassuring welcome, the man had sent back a message stating his visit was expected.

The trek to Uisdein was just over a day, travel was over land until arriving at the northern shores of South Uist. From there they would be transported across by ships that were sturdy enough to include the horses.

Upon arriving, Darach and his ten guards were allowed past the gates into the courtyard. It had been a long time since he'd been there, only once had he accompanied his father, who'd traveled there several times, but never brought him or his brothers along.

From the entrance to his home, Laird Uisdein greeted him, along with who he assumed were councilmen.

Once in the great hall, he was invited to sit at a table that had been prepared for him. There were platters of food and pitchers filled to the rim with ale. Breads and cheese trays were placed on each end of the table along with plates of fruit.

"Welcome, young Laird," The Uisdein said, his words not exactly warm. The man was quite a bit older than him, with red hair, bushy brows, and cold assessing blue eyes. By his girth, he seemed to enjoy food and rest quite a bit. The man's round stomach protruded so much he seemed to lean back when standing and walking.

"Thank ye for yer hospitality," Darach replied sitting, but not touching anything on the table. He caught several of the men, exchanging conspirator glances, which gave him pause.

"My men will remain outside the gates. They bring their own provisions." Darach had instructed the men, not to venture from their horses and keep his close as well.

"Of course," the laird said motioning a servant nearby. "I assure ye, we can house them and their steeds."

"They will sleep in the field just outside the gates," Darach said. "We do not wish to burden ye with having to house us and our steeds as this will not be a long visit."

If the man was insulted at his refusal of hospitality, he did not show it. "Very well."

Once everyone sat, the Uisdein met his gaze. "Yer father and I had come to several agreements that he and ye have not held to."

The man did not waste time and in a way, Darach was glad for it. He was not in the mood to play political games. "I am not aware of any agreements. Father did not tell me, or the council about it."

"Then allow me to enlighten ye," the man said with a

scowl. "Yer father agreed to provide a hundred men. We were to fight against the Macdonald and overtake them. It seems interesting to me that ye married one as soon as yer father died."

Darach slid a look to the door, two guards stood in front of it. On the opposite side of the room, another pair of guards blocked that exit.

"As I said, I was not aware of any kind of agreements. Ye ended my brother's betrothal with yer daughter without explanation. Ye sent messengers back without any word."

The Uisdein shifted in his seat, his narrowed eyes moving from the food to Darach. "Do ye reject the offerings?" The man motioned to a servant who poured ale into everyone's goblet.

Only after the man next to him drank did Darach. The motion did not go unnoticed by the Uisdein who sneered.

"If ye and Father were to overtake the Macdonald, what would my father have to gain from it? Yer lands border theirs, we are further south."

When the man chuckled, it was as if he considered Darach to be too daft to understand. "Rights to an entire Isle. Rich fishing, hunting, and plenty of access further north."

Once the man spoke, Darach knew that unless he swore alliance, he would not leave with the knowledge of what the Uisdein planned to do.

With the four guards by the doors and the six men at the table, it would be impossible for him to get away. Four men, he could fight and perhaps have a chance, but ten was too many.

"I do not agree with what ye plan. My marriage to a Macdonald has nothing to do with any of yer plotting."

"Yer father was a traitor. Or perhaps the marriage was part of the plan. Since he fell ill and his messenger never came, we will never know."

Darach's gut tightened. "Messenger?"

"Cairn McKinney."

"Of course."

"Eat," the Uisdein said motioning to the trays of food. "Ye must be hungry after the long travel."

Darach searched for a way to figure out how to get away from the room. "I will have to ask for privacy to see about my needs."

"Of course," the Uisdein said motioning to the guards. "Assist the laird to a place of privacy."

The four guards surrounded him One yanking the sword from his scabbard another yanking his dirk from his belt. There was a third one in his boot, which they did not search as he was grabbed by the arms.

Darach hit one in the stomach and kicked another. He managed to land several punches, but there were too many against him and soon he fell to the floor bleeding and winded.

"We will speak more once yer men have been dealt with," Uisdein called out as he was taken, struggling and kicking.

CHAPTER SIXTEEN

M EN WENT IN and out of Darach's study. More than usual and Isobel couldn't help but wonder if something was afoot. Duncan, whom she didn't know well at all, kept to himself when not at the great hall hearing grievances.

The man was imposing and of all the brothers, the one she considered the most standoffish. Poor Beatrice practically raced to hide whenever he came around.

She knocked on the study door and walked in after a deep voice called out, "Enter."

Duncan's gaze met hers for a moment. "Lady Ross." He had two-colored eyes, like her brother Evander, both had brown right eyes, Duncan's left hazel. Evander's left eye was blue.

"Please call me Isobel."

"Very well, what can I help ye with, Isobel."

Duncan was the opposite of Darach. Deep brown hair and tan skin, he looked like a man who spent most of his days out of doors. Although muscular in build, his movements were graceful when he stood and motioned for her to sit. The man was like a giant, a head taller than his brothers and shoulders so wide, she wondered how he fit through most doorways.

"Have ye received any message from Darach? I expected he would have returned by now."

"I have." Duncan stood and rounded the table, then lowered to a chair near hers. "A messenger arrived a short time ago."

Isobel's stomach sank, but she refused to panic. "Is he remaining longer then?"

"Just a couple days," he replied and looked to the doorway. "I was just about to inform ye and Mother."

Something about his demeanor gave Isobel pause. Sure, she didn't know him well and perhaps, not enough to read him. In her gut, Isobel sensed he held something back.

"Did the messenger say anything else?"

"Nay," Duncan replied. He seemed ill at ease, and she wondered if perhaps it was because he was a reclusive sort, not one to care to be around people.

Isobel cared little about how he felt in that moment. She locked gazes with him. "Is my husband safe at this moment?"

When his jaw flexed, she knew immediately something was wrong. "Where is Darach?"

"He is being held by the Uisdein. The man is angry over a disagreement with our late father. It will be resolved with haste."

"Ye were not going to tell me?"

"No need to have hysterical women about right now."

She curled her fingers into a fist and pushed her hand into the pocket of her dress to keep from striking the infuriating man. "I have every right to know if my husband is in danger. Do not dare keep any information from me. What are ye planning to do?"

With an annoyed groan, the man stood and stalked from the room.

Isobel ran after him. "Duncan! Duncan, tell me what ye are planning."

Lady Mariel came when hearing her and looked to her son. "Is something amiss?"

Duncan took his mother's arm and walked with her to the dining room, Isobel on their heels. "Mother, I have to deal with a situation. I do not want to have to explain my actions to ye or her." He motioned to Isobel with his head.

Stuart, Ewan, and Gideon entered the room. The brothers stopped upon seeing her and their mother.

"What happened to my son?" Lady Mariel asked. Her face paled when the silence stretched. "Tell me or I swear to beat ye each to within an inch of life."

It was Stuart who spoke. "The Uisdein took Darach prisoner. We are to ride there with half our army to rescue him."

"Ye know very well, if ye attack, he will not be kept alive," Lady Mariel said shocking everyone into silence. "Duncan, send a messenger asking that the laird meet ye on neutral land. Each of ye brings fifty men, no more. Insist that Darach and his guardsmen be brought alive. Be sure to let him know that if he is not present at the meeting place at the time allotted, we will attack."

Duncan gave his mother a flat look. "Thank ye for yer advice," he replied in a flat tone, telling her it was exactly what they were in the midst of doing. Preparations that were being made were for the meeting that was about to take place.

Gideon gave their mother an indulgent smile. "We do not give women enough credence. Ye are quite intelligent, Mother."

"Stop speaking and go see about my son," Lady Mariel

snapped. "Which one of ye remains back?"

"Caelan comes to take my place," Duncan said.

For the next hour, Isobel kept track of every activity, following what they did and what everyone said. If all went well, the Ross brothers would return with Darach within three days.

It would be the longest three days of her life.

She ducked into an alcove and leaned against the wall. A heavy pain constricted her chest. If Darach was injured or dead, would she sense it? Tears stung, and she pushed away from the wall doing her best to blink them away.

Through sheer willpower, she fought not to break down, there was too much to ensure was done right.

Already healers had been summoned, some would follow the men to the Uisdein lands. Hundreds of men and horses filled the field just outside the gates, the air ripe with a sense of what could come. Some men would remain behind to guard the keep, others would ride with the Ross brothers to face their enemy.

If a battle ensued, not all would return.

Her gut in knots, Isobel hurried toward the kitchens where food was being prepared and packed for the large contingency of men that were about to travel. The activity was dizzying, but soon Isobel joined the throng of women cooking, cutting, and wrapping food items and packing them into wooden crates that would be loaded onto a large wagon.

Lads rushed past the doorway with bundles of blankets and others with sacks filled with bandages and ointments.

Isobel finished packing a crate just as Ella appeared at the door and motioned for her.

"What happens?" Isobel asked catching up to Ella who

rushed down the corridor. They went up the stairs to the sitting room where Lady Mariel and Beatrice sat. They were drinking tea while cutting sheets into strips for bandages.

"Sit," Lady Mariel said, motioning to a chair. "I do not want ye exhausting yerself. When Darach returns, he will need ye to be strong and help him with whatever is needed."

Isobel fought the urge to tell her mother-in-law, sitting about would drive her crazy. Instead, she grabbed several strips and began rolling them while standing near the door.

"All will be well. I am sure the Uisdein does not wish to go to war. Our army is much larger than his."

Isobel's heart lifted. "Is that true?"

"It is," Ella replied. "The reason we've not had war in a long time is because our enemy's armies are both smaller. If they formed an alliance, even then, we would be just a wee bit larger."

"There will not be a war," Lady Mariel said, her face drawn with worry.

Just then shouts sounded and as a group, they rushed out of the room and up the stairs to the top of the building. From there, they could see the huge contingency of men. The warriors formed four straight long lines.

From the regalia of the horses, it was easy to make out the Ross brothers, each mounted in front of a line of men.

Duncan lifted his arm, and everyone called out, what Isobel knew as the clan creed. After, that he rode out with his group of men.

One by one, Stuart, Ewan, and Gideon each followed with a line of men behind.

If she counted right, each brother had fifty warriors for a

total of two hundred men. The ones who remained behind stood in four lines of the same number, before them on his horse was Caelan, who rode between the flanks speaking to them.

"My sons, Darach and Caelan included, are all strong and noble men. I am very proud of them all." Lady Mariel gave a sad sigh.

"Where is Caelan's mother?" Beatrice asked peering down at the large man.

Her name is Celia, and she lives in one of the villages with her husband.

"Ye had her thrown out then?" Beatrice asked and Isobel didn't bother correcting her. She was too busy watching the men ride into the distance.

Lady Mariel shook her head. "No. I do not believe Celia wished to lay with my husband or bear his child. She is now married to a man she loves dearly."

"Oh," Beatrice replied. "He was not a kind man at all then?"

"Not in the least," Lady Mariel replied.

Lady Mariel came to Isobel and hugged her waist. "We must have faith that all will be well and Darach will return to us safely. Ye cannot leave any room for worry or doubt."

"How can ye be so strong? The Macdonalds have never been at war in North Uist, not for decades. I do not know what it is to see so many men formed together and ride off to battle."

Lady Mariel looked to Ella. "I am strong for my children. Even though they are all full-grown adults, they remain mine to pray for and look after. Motherhood never ends."

When the last of the men rode out of sight, they made their way back downstairs. Lady Mariel hurried across the great hall with Isobel following.

She entered the kitchen and looked to the head cook. "Greer, will the guardsmen take care of meals for the men outside?"

The cook nodded. "Aye. The baker from the village will be sending bread. Boars will be roasted, and pottage is being boiled over a fire in the courtyard."

"Very good," her mother-in-law went to a side table. "A simple meal of bread and cheese will suffice for last meal for us. There are only five of us inside the keep."

"I willna hear of it," the cook replied. "We are roasting a chicken with vegetables for ye." The woman made shooing motions. "Go on and do what ye need. Last meal will be ready at the normal time."

After offering thanks and a warm smile to the cook, Lady Mariel got a bone with bits of meat on it and walked from the room.

"Where is Albie?" She went to the great hall to find Darach's dog sleeping near the hearth. The dog wagged its tail but did not show interest in the tasty offering.

Isobel kneeled next to the animal. "What is it boy? Ye love bones."

"He does not care for Darach to be gone so long," Lady Mariel said. "I have tried to urge him to eat since yesterday."

"I will help," Isobel said. "I think he will enjoy a walk."

"Do not go far," Lady Mariel said already rushing to whatever the next task was.

"Come Albie," Isobel called motioning to the dog, who

rushed to her side. They walked out into the courtyard and on through the side gates to where she and Darach had walked together with Albie before.

The excited dog ran to find a stick, while Isobel stood, looking off toward the sea. It was so utterly unnecessary for there to be constant conflict. Why couldn't people remain satisfied with what they had? It was as if certain men fought for power, not caring about the cost to their people or realizing the fact that nothing in life was permanent. Sooner or later, the power-hungry men would die, and all the strife would not stop it.

Albie appeared from the edge of the woods with a much too large branch. The pup struggled to drag it toward her, and she couldn't keep from laughing. Taking pity on it, she hurried to grab the branch, broke off a piece, and gave it to Albie, who ran in a circle.

Although the dog was happy in the moment, like her, once back inside, they would feel the emptiness from Darach being gone.

"Ye should not be this far out," the unfamiliar voice made Isobel swing around. Caelan stood a few feet away. She couldn't keep from taking in the man.

Despite Darach being blond, the resemblance between him and his brothers was obvious. They all had hazel eyes and the same strong chin. There was something about them too that was similar, in their stance and build.

Caelan however, was nothing like the others. His features were aristocratic, a slender patrician nose, and his almond-shaped eyes were blue. Caelan's rich auburn hair was sheered to just below his jawline and combed back away from his face.

He was of good stature, but not as broad as his brothers. Of all of them, he had a regal air, as if he were nobility.

Isobel had to admit to finding the man intriguing. For whatever reason, he rarely visited the keep. According to Darach, it was because he had been cast away to live in the other home since a child and was therefore not as close to the others.

When Duncan had also been asked to leave, he'd gone to live with Caelan, it was only since then that the brothers had gotten to know Caelan better.

"When do ye think they will return?" Isobel asked, not moving, keeping a watch on Albie.

"There is no way to know exactly. I do feel that once the Uisdein sees the size of our army, and that we do not expect to be challenged, he will relent immediately."

Isobel closed her eyes. She wanted to ask the most pressing question on her mind but was terrified.

"My brother is unharmed. It would not be in the Uisdein's interest to hurt him in any manner."

At his words, she turned away and wiped an errant tear. Her husband was in danger. Just the thought that he could be killed sent painful stabs all through her body. If she were to be honest, it was hard to fathom what would happen if he never returned. Her mind refused to go to that place, the dark corner of fear.

"I do not know ye very well. I do not know Darach very well for that matter," Isobel said making her way back to the keep. "In what birth order do ye fall?"

Caelan knew that she tried to distract herself by the understanding look he gave her.

"I am the same age as Duncan, he is older by only a couple of weeks actually. Darach is the eldest, followed by Duncan and me, then Stuart, finally there's Ewan, then Gideon, and the youngest is Ella."

"There are so many of ye," Isobel said with a smile. "There are only four of us. My brothers are older than Beatrice and me. She is the youngest."

He looked to the keep as if considering it for the first time. "I am sure yer father is very different than mine."

Not one to keep from the truth, Isobel nodded. "From what I've heard, aye. My father is kind and dotes on our mother, my sister, and me. My brothers and our father get along as well." She paused in thought. "I wish every marriage would be like my parents'."

"Perhaps if people stopped insisting on arranging marriages between strangers." Caelan met her gaze. "If I were ever to marry, it will be the woman whom I choose."

Isobel chuckled. "And hopefully chooses ye in return?"

"Of course," he replied.

She liked Caelan. Although just meeting, it was effortless to feel at ease with him. Isobel hated that he didn't feel comfortable enough to remain at the keep for longer visits. She was sure they would become fast friends.

"Yer sister should be able to return home once Darach is back."

"I will inform her. Although to be honest, I wish she would stay longer. I will miss her terribly. She and Ella have become fast friends as well."

She gave Caelan a teasing look. "Have ye met her?"

"I have briefly." The corner of his mouth lifted acknowledging he knew what she was up to.

They walked a bit longer in silence until reaching the gates. Isobel touched his forearm. "Thank ye for setting my mind at ease. I feel much better."

Isobel called for Albie to follow and she headed to the kitchen entrance. She hoped to retrieve the meaty bone so that the dog would eat.

"If ye would add some honey, oats, and perhaps a bit of chopped apple, it would make for a marvelous pudding..." Beatrice, who stood atop a chair stirring a huge pot, looked over and brightened at seeing Isobel.

She neared and sniffed at what smelled to be spiced porridge. "What are ye doing?"

"Making food for the men. This is much better than that insufferable pottage they are making out there."

Always bothering their cook at home, Beatrice was indeed a good cook in her own right. Isobel neared. "It certainly smells delicious."

Greer looked on from the table with a pleased smile. "It isn't often that I am ordered to sit and rest while someone takes over the kitchen duties."

Moments later, Beatrice climbed down from the chair and hugged Isobel. "Any news?"

"No," Isobel replied. "I spoke to Caelan, and he gave me reassurance that Darach would be returned unharmed once Laird Uisdein sees the size of the army outside his keep."

"And well he should. Although it would probably be a good idea to attack once he does. Teach him a lesson."

"Beatrice!" Isobel's eyes rounded. "That would be horrible."

"I do not agree," her sister said with a firm nod. "Men like him need a good reminder of what could happen if they continue down certain paths."

Not sure what to say, Isobel looked to Greer who was no help as she'd fallen asleep. When she turned to the doorway, Caelan stood there with a soft smile.

"I find I agree with ye Miss Beatrice. A good lesson would be my choice if I were Duncan."

Interesting combination, Isobel thought, her sister and Caelan Ross. Both intelligent and perhaps Beatrice's playful nature would be a good balance to Caelan's reclusive one.

"Beatrice, Caelan informed me that he and Duncan are the same age."

Her sister looked to the man for a moment. "Ye seem younger."

"Why is that?"

"It could be that ye dress more like an Englishman than a Scot."

Isobel coughed at Beatrice's words. Admittedly, she'd thought the same thing, but would never say it out loud.

To her surprise, Caelan burst out laughing. "It could be because I lived in the south for so long that I dress like they do. I assure ye I own a plaid and plenty of woolen tunics."

Her sister gave him a once-over, then climbed back onto the chair. "The porridge will be done soon." She looked to a lad who sat on a stool waiting for instructions. "Go fetch a pair of men to help carry this out."

"I will scoop out some for us," Isobel said noting Caelan remained. He was studying her sister with curiosity. "Would ye like some pudding, Caelan?"

"Aye, I would."

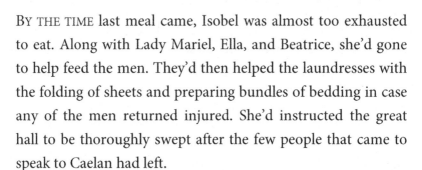

BY THE TIME last meal came, Isobel was almost too exhausted to eat. Along with Lady Mariel, Ella, and Beatrice, she'd gone to help feed the men. They'd then helped the laundresses with the folding of sheets and preparing bundles of bedding in case any of the men returned injured. She'd instructed the great hall to be thoroughly swept after the few people that came to speak to Caelan had left.

He along with the council had spent the afternoon speaking to the warriors and inspecting the horses. She'd caught Beatrice watching him as he helped lads carry firewood into the house. During times like these, there was no time for idleness.

Isobel trudged up the stairs and into her and Darach's bedchamber. Annis walked in with her. "There is hot water in the pitcher and clean cloths on the stand." She went to a trunk and pulled out a nightdress. "I will help ye get ready for bed."

After undressing, Isobel washed away the dirt of the day. She then sat so that Annis could brush her hair out. "Will ye stay a moment and pray with me?" Isobel asked.

"Of course."

She prayed fervently until tears streamed down her cheeks. "Ye need to rest," Annis said helping her to bed.

In the darkness, she reached for the opposite side of the bed. It was so very cold.

CHAPTER SEVENTEEN

D ARACH STALKED FROM one side of the room to the other. He stopped occasionally and peered through the window. Several times he'd gauged the possibility of climbing out of it. Although he could climb halfway down, the fall from there was too high and he'd probably break a leg.

The room faced the courtyard, so it would be impossible to escape using bedding without being caught. Besides, the damn Uisdein had thought of everything and had guards posted outside his door and two more below the window.

With an annoyed grunt, he looked up at the sky, noting that it was quite clear, the moon full and bright.

His jaw ached from the blows the day before and earlier that evening, when he'd rushed the man who'd brought him last meal. He had made it past him, but the guards at the door had not been as easy to get through.

Several blows were thrown, and unfortunately, he was the recipient of most.

Duncan would send an army for him. Once the Uisdein saw, he would either have him executed and declare war, or he would accede to discussions.

Although not afraid of death, he couldn't help but think of Isobel. Once married, a man's perspective changed. Before he would have fought to the death, not caring about more than what damage he could cause his opponent.

This time, however, when fighting the guards, he'd held back upon realizing he would not win. Not because he didn't want to be injured, but because he wished to return to Isobel.

Angry at the situation, he went to the bed and lay atop the bedding fully dressed.

If what he expected was to be, as soon as the sun rose, the view from his window would be quite impressive.

AT THE SOUNDS of raised voices, Darach jumped from the bed and rushed to the window. Throwing the drapes aside, he peered out, and his lips curved. The sun rose in the horizon giving him a clear view.

For as far as he could see, lines of men on horseback, evenly spaced apart, faced the keep. In the front were four horsemen, who he recognized as Stuart, Duncan, Ewan, and Gideon. His brothers made a point to stand out, their horses draped with the Ross colors, and they each wore their tartans, wrapped around their waists and over the left shoulder.

Behind each of his brothers were four warriors. Two armed with claymores and two archers. It was all a show of force and more for intimidation than practicality. Archers were normally kept to the rear and warriors, swords drawn, in front.

The entire army held swords or other weapons, prepared for battle. A fight he hoped would not come to be.

The Uisdein guard stood shoulder to shoulder atop the keep walls, while others mounted war horses in the courtyard.

It occurred to Darach that the Uisdein was not at all prepared. By his count, there were only about fifty men and horses in addition to another perhaps twenty atop the wall. What had the man expected?

That Clan Ross would not retaliate at him being taken by force?

"What an idiot," he mumbled. After pushing the window frame and finding it nailed shut, he took a chair and broke the glass. Leaning out, he waved to his brothers.

Duncan saw him first and waved back.

The guards outside the chamber door kicked it open and burst into the room, swords drawn. Turning from the window, Darach gave them a droll look.

"Do ye bring me something to break my fast?" he asked, looking at the broken dishes from the night before. "Some ale, perhaps."

A guard neared but didn't attack. "My laird requests yer presence. Immediately."

"Is that so?"

"Come with us."

He took his time walking to the door and then looked at the guards who stood in the corridor until they parted and allowed him to walk past.

There were groups of people sheltered in the great hall. Women with children huddled together in groups, sheltering from the possibility of an attack.

A small boy rushed up to him and spit at his feet, then ran away screaming. Darach looked to the mother, whose eyes widened. "He will be a great warrior one day."

The woman's look of surprise was replaced with pride. She

nodded.

"Continue on. My laird is outside," a guard barked but did not touch him. Interesting how an army outside one's gates changes things.

They continued until out in the courtyard. "Yer horse is saddled and ready," one guard said in a flat tone.

"What about my men?"

"They await ye outside the gate."

Laird Uisdein flanked by two men waited, his flat gaze meeting his. He gave a nod, as greeting. Darach didn't respond.

When Darach walked over to the Uisdein, the men beside the laird moved to block him. Although Darach had not met the two who shielded the man, he assumed them to be his sons by their age and similar hair color.

"I have no sword, nor do I have the need to hurt him," he told the two.

He pinned the laird with a straight look. "Although, I must admit to the urge to punch ye in the face."

Uisdein pushed past his sons. "We should talk. There has been a misunderstanding on my part, I am sure. Perhaps the agreement between yer father and I can be reassessed."

"There will not be an agreement between us to do anything against my wife's clan."

"Once a pact is made, between lairds, it should be adhered to. Otherwise…"

Before anyone could stop him, Darach launched at the man, grabbing him by the tunic and pulling him close. When the sons tried to interfere, the Uisdein gave them a look, and they stood back.

"Listen to me well," Darach said, his face a scant breath between them. "I do not wish to discuss anything further with ye. Know that by taking me against my will, we are now enemies. One misstep and I will not hesitate to release my army against ye."

The man's nose flared. "Ye came so that we could talk."

"I did, but now there will be no talking between us. Ye are a fool." Darach pushed the man away and stalked to his horse. The Uisdein and his sons rushed to do the same.

The laird came alongside, his face red with fury. However, unless he wished to insult his brothers, it was customary for him to ride out in a show of goodwill.

When the Uisdein motioned for it, the guards opened the gates, and together as a group, they rode through them and stopped.

Darach's chest swelled with pride at seeing his clan's men, prepared to fight for his freedom.

The Uisdein's gaze narrowed at Darach. "We do not fear ye."

"Ye should," Darach motioned out to where his army was. "That is not half of them."

The Uisdein's eyes widened just a bit before he managed to rein in his reaction. The stubborn idiot huffed and did not reply.

"Perhaps we can meet at another time and talk," one of the men beside the laird suggested.

Darach met his gaze. "I have no idea who ye are. Yer laird did not extend the courtesy even now to introduce ye, so ye must be of little importance." The younger man's jaw tightened, but he remained silent.

"My stance does not change," Darach continued. "I do not consider ye allies, yer clan cannot depend on Clan Ross for any support."

The Uisdein men exchanged looks and the laird looked to him. "This is not over young laird. Ye will learn sooner or later that this is a game of power. Those who are clever enough to gain it, in the end, will win."

"It is beliefs like yers that bring death and destruction to our people. In the end, what price do ye pay for gaining personal power? Death, deprivation, and people who hate and fear ye. Is that the kind price ye wish to pay?"

Without waiting for a reply, Darach urged his mount forward to where the men who'd come with him waited.

"Let us go," he called out to them, and together, he and his men, who looked as tired as he felt, then rode to where his brothers awaited.

"Brother," Duncan said taking him in. The others remained silent; however, it was easy to tell they were glad to see him as each one took a moment to look him over before seeming satisfied he was not injured too badly.

"We should attack and burn the keep to the ground," Stuart said between clenched teeth.

"I agree," Darach replied. "However, we will not."

His brothers waited for his orders as to what they would do next. "We will not attack, despite the fact I do not think this is over. The man is hungry for power at any cost."

"Perhaps a good lesson would quell it a bit?" Gideon said, glaring toward the keep.

"I may regret this, but no. We will wait."

Gideon, Stuart, and Ewan turned their horses around and

began shouting out orders for retreat. The flanks of men parted to allow Darach and Duncan to ride through to the front. Only once they were safely protected by the men behind them, would the warriors follow.

Duncan grunted. "What reason did he give for imprisoning ye?"

"He is angry that we did not keep to an agreement he and Da had made."

"A plan?"

"Aye, they were to attack the Macdonald and split the lands, livestock, and whatever else they found."

His brother gave him an incredulous look. "It would never have worked. The Macdonalds are allied to the MacLeod, together they are twice as powerful as us."

"I do not understand either," Darach said. "With Cairn missing, I am not sure who else would know how they planned to accomplish this."

As much as he wanted to ask about Isobel, Darach realized his brother would not know much more than him. He'd barely been gone two days before a messenger had been sent about his capture.

"I'm hungry," he murmured. "Have anything?"

Duncan yanked some dried meat from a sack and handed him a wineskin. "He didn't feed ye?"

"They did, but I was not about to eat and be poisoned."

They rode for a bit, Darach taking in the scenery. "I wonder if the Uisdein is under threat and that is the reason he wanted this agreement. To gain our alliance."

"It was an idiotic way to go about it," Duncan replied.

"We must send spies and find out exactly what is happening."

His brother nodded. After spending many years on ships and traveling, Duncan knew men who would take on such a task. His solemn brother had many secrets that he kept to himself. Darach hoped one day to find out more.

"I wish to spend time with ye Duncan. Caelan as well. Perhaps I can get away from my duties this winter and come to visit for a week or two."

"Ye are always welcome," Duncan replied without inflection.

When his stomach growled, Darach chewed the meat and washed it down with wine. "Do ye know anyone who Cairn would confide in?"

"There is a guard who I saw at the tavern with Cairn once. I am not sure why I hadn't considered that he would probably be who freed him."

"Which one is it?"

"Young man, I believe his name is Jon or James. Has reddish hair, freckled face."

Darach knew who Duncan referred to. If it was James McTavish, the guard would be punished. McTavish had a young wife and a wee bairn, just born.

"He must have dangled plenty of coin in front of him. I can't imagine James McTavish being tempted. Although I suppose a wife and wee one can make a man susceptible."

"What will ye do?"

"Question him. Find out as much as we can. Toss him in the dungeon for a month."

Duncan grunted in agreement.

At the thought of a bairn, Darach considered something he

needed to do. While imprisoned, he'd thought about the possibility of dying and leaving behind a bairn. He needed to find out the truth.

"I have something to do," Darach said. "I must speak to Lilia. Return to the keep. Let them know I am well. I will be there before last meal."

"Is it a good idea?" Duncan asked. "Perhaps ye can go after."

"This is something I need to find out. I will not be long."

After a moment, Duncan met his gaze. "Why do ye seek out Lilia?"

"She is with child. If the bairn is mine, I need to know."

"Very well, aye. Take some men with ye," Duncan finally relented.

If LILIA WAS surprised to see him, she didn't act it. "Ye come alone. Already ye grow bored of her?"

Darach didn't want to make her angry as he hoped to find out the truth. While at the Uisdein and wondering if he'd live, one of the things he'd wanted to know was if he would have left a child.

"Did a midwife come to see ye?" he asked.

Lilia met his gaze, her lips curving. "Why would one come? It will not be time for a few months yet." She walked to him and wrapped her arms around his waist then leaned her head on his chest. "I miss ye terribly, my laird."

"Ye should marry and have yer own family," Darach said. "I can arrange it."

When she didn't reply, Darach hugged her back. The woman had been kind to him and warmed his bed many a night. He didn't love her. However, he'd grown fond of her and felt responsible to ensure she was protected, even if not carrying his child.

"Lilia, I wish for ye to be provided for."

"Ye can keep me here, come spend time with me…"

"I cannot." He lifted her chin so she could look at him. "Is the bairn mine?"

Her gaze fell, and for a long moment, he wondered if she was to reply. "Nay."

Relief filled him.

"Allow me to help ye, Lilia."

"No one will have me. I am not the kind of woman a man marries." When she began to cry, he felt bad for her.

"I will find ye a willing husband, a good man. What of the bairn's father?"

She shook her head but said nothing.

"Then I will ensure ye are protected."

He kissed her brow and met her gaze. "Be with care, Lilia."

By her resigned expression, she was aware he'd never seek her out again.

CHAPTER EIGHTEEN

AT THE MEN returning, Isobel gathered with Lady Mariel, Ella, and Beatrice to welcome Darach back. Already a scout had arrived to announce that everything had gone smoothly. Darach had ridden out of the Uisdein keep relatively unscathed.

The gates opened and the brothers rode in, behind them several guards.

"Thank God," Lady Mariel said, then looked to Isobel puzzled. "Do ye see Darach?"

Already Isobel had noticed his absence and held her hands to her chest. "Why is he not with them? Could it be the scout was mistaken?"

The brothers dismounted, but only Duncan walked to them. The others darted looks toward the women and seemed reluctant to enter the keep.

"What happened?" Both Isobel and Lady Mariel asked in unison. Lady Mariel grabbed Duncan's arm. "Tell me, son."

With an annoyed expression, Duncan met Isobel's gaze and then pulled his mother against his side. "Darach is fine. He went to the village to see about something. He will be here for last meal."

"The village?" Lady Mariel gave her son an incredulous look. "Why would he go to the village?"

Isobel instantly knew. He'd gone to see Lilia first upon being released. Of course. A man in love who thought he might die would want reassurance from the most important person in his life.

Whirling on her heel, she ran past the great hall and up the stairs. Effective immediately, she would not be sharing a room with him. It was enough to be humiliated in such a way, but to then act as if nothing happened and share a bed with him each night was not in her nature.

"Isobel?" Beatrice walked into the room. "What are ye doing?"

"Do ye not see? I am packing my belongings. Please call Annis. I am moving into the empty bedchamber across the corridor."

"Are ye sure," Beatrice asked. "I am sure he has a reasonable explanation."

Unable to keep her anger in check, she met her sister's gaze. "What do ye suppose he is doing at the village? Drinking at the pub with old friends?"

"It could be he needs to know about the bairn."

"I do not care why he went there. What matters is that he wished to go straight to her upon being freed. Not here to me, or to his family home, but directly to the woman who may be carrying his child."

Annis must have been alerted because she hurried in and without a word began pulling her gowns from the wardrobe and taking them to the bedchamber across the corridor.

"Oh, Isobel. I am so very sorry," Beatrice said. "I had hoped ye would be in a love match. He seems besotted by ye."

Her heart ached, but she fought tears. "I expected this

would happen. I'd hoped it would not hurt as much as it does. However, I am sure, over the years, it will become easier."

While they worked, Lady Mariel walked in. "Oh no, darling, ye should not do this. Wait to speak to Darach. There could be a good explanation."

"Such as?" Isobel lifted a basket filled with her hair accessories and other items to her hip. "After being freed from captivity, is there any explanation for going straight to another woman than love?"

Lady Mariel blew out a breath. "I suppose not. It could be he was worried about her state."

"Lady Mariel, I appreciate ye standing up for yer son." Isobel allowed Annis to take the basket and met her mother-in-law's gaze. "In my place, what would ye do? I cannot bear sharing the same bed with him each night. Not after he leaves hers. How can ye possible ask me to?"

Unable to keep from it, Isobel began to cry allowing Lady Mariel to hold her close. "I am so very sorry for this. I would not ever have expected him to disrespect ye in such a manner."

Together they went to the other chamber. Isobel could not bear to remain in the one she'd shared with Darach any longer. Her entire body ached, every limb weak and shaky. She realized she had not eaten since the day before and now it felt impossible.

"I wish to lie down for a bit. I do not feel well." She undressed, dropping her clothes to the floor, not caring who watched and slid between the blankets.

Beatrice climbed on the bed and snuggled next to her. Soon the room was quiet, everyone had gone except her sister, who cried softly next to her.

VOICES WOKE ISOBEL much later, the room was dark meaning she'd slept for hours. At first, she was confused as to where she was, but then recalling the events of the day, she closed her eyes not wishing to face whatever came next.

It sounded as if Darach was arguing with someone, another male, Duncan perhaps, just outside the door.

Darach was midsentence. "...and my wife will not..."

"Ye cannot demand anything right now," Duncan said and then grumbled something else in a lower tone, so Isobel could not hear.

The door opened and Isobel closed her eyes, pretending to sleep.

Beatrice sat up. "What are ye doing?"

"I need to speak to Isobel," Darach said in a quiet voice.

"As ye can see, she is asleep," her sister whispered.

There was a beat of silence. "Please leave us."

"No." Beatrice's tone left no room for argument.

After a few beats, footsteps retreated, and the door closed.

"Arse," Beatrice said with a huff.

"Thank ye," Isobel said softly in case Darach was outside the door. "I do not think I can face him today."

Last meal was brought to her by Annis who lit a lantern and set up a table with an embroidered cloth. The three of them, Isobel, Beatrice, and Annis ate the food. Everything smelled delicious and yet to Isobel, it tasted bland.

All she wished to do was return to bed. "I am not sure when I will feel up to facing people again," she told her companions. "I am so humiliated."

"Everyone will act as if they do not know, I'm sure," Beatrice said. "They have to, ye are the lady of the house."

"What are the servants saying Annis?" Isobel met her companion's anxious gaze. "Tell me the truth."

Annis closed her eyes for a moment, and Isobel knew what she was about to say would be hurtful. "They are saying that the laird sought Lilia's bed, preferring her to ye."

"Oh." The spoon fell from Isobel's hand, landing with a thump on the tabletop.

Beatrice took her hand. "It will be fine. As much as I hate to say it, this is a common occurrence and not something that diminishes yer marriage in the eyes of the clan."

"Of course, it does," Isobel said. "It may not affect him in any way, after all, men are given so much leave when it comes to infidelity. I, however, will be seen as someone who cannot satisfy her husband. Unable to keep him in my bed."

Once they finished eating, Isobel asked for both of the women to leave. She brushed the tangles from her hair out and paced the room. Although smaller than the bedchamber she'd shared with Darach, it was a good size.

The canopied bed was large enough for two people. There was also a dressing table, a screen in the corner of the room, and a small wardrobe.

Next to the window was a washstand and a chair, all in all, it was a bedchamber that would serve her well.

From this window, she had a different view than the one across the corridor. Instead of the field and forest, this room faced out to a craggy mountain that sloped down until meeting the sea. The moonlight gave it just a beautiful dusting of light that, under other circumstances, she would immediately pull out her chalks and sketch.

Not wishing to prolong her first night alone, Isobel returned to the bed. The sooner she fell asleep, the better.

THE NEXT DAY, dressed in one of her brown dresses, Isobel went down the stairs and past the great hall. She'd eaten first and midday meals in her room, to avoid having to sit at the high board next to Darach. The buzz in the room quieted when she passed, but she managed to keep her head up and gaze focused on the exterior of the building.

"Isobel." It was Stuart who came up to her.

Turning to meet his eyes, she ensured to keep a flat expression. "What is it?"

"Darach wishes to speak to ye in private."

"Tell him I cannot at this moment. I am going for a walk. Alone." Not waiting for a reply, she walked away praying no one followed. It turned out Albie followed. The dog walked alongside her, his tongue hanging out of his mouth. He looked to be smiling and she envied him.

Without a sketchbook, Isobel climbed up to her perch and looked across the Ross lands. This day was different. Unlike the sunny days before, the cloudy skies matched her current mood.

How was she to carry on? Isobel wished there was a way to know how long before the ache in her chest and stomach would go away. Lady Mariel would probably have some insight, when she could bring herself to ask.

From what she understood, however, Lady Mariel never

loved her husband. It would have been so much easier for her. Isobel had not been as smart. So many times, she'd reminded herself not to allow Darach to enter her heart, but from the pain in her chest, it had been an impossible task.

In the distance, a large wagon, pulled by two horses, ambled up the road toward the keep. All kinds of wares hung from the sides and the wooden frame was covered by thick fabric.

A well-stocked peddler.

From what Ella had said, the peddler who came every month carried all sorts of hard-to-find items. Beatrice and she had been waiting for him impatiently. Now here he was, on the day that she cared little for anything.

Isobel didn't move, her gaze following the wagon that entered through the gates. When she threw a stick for Albie, he lost interest and raced after the wagon.

Later when she walked past, Beatrice tried to convince her to go look at the peddler's offerings.

Her pretty face was flushed with excitement. "He has items I have never seen. Beautiful combs and ribbons. I am sure it will be a good distraction for ye."

"Go, enjoy yerself. I have a headache and need to rest. Soon it will be last meal." Isobel hurried through the great hall and up the stairs. Then she went directly to the sitting room only to find it empty. Of course, Lady Mariel and Ella were probably at the peddler's wagon.

When she walked into her new bedchamber, she regretted it as Darach walked in after her.

"We should talk."

Just the sound of his voice sent trickles of fury up and

down her spine. Isobel shuddered when she looked up to him. "About what?"

"I wish to explain why I went to the village directly after leaving Uisdein."

Isobel didn't want to hear a word. What she wanted was for him to leave her be and not speak to her for a long, long time.

She let out a harsh breath. "It is clear, Laird. Ye do not have to explain. What led ye directly to her is love."

"Love?" He neared and reached to lift her chin, but she backed away.

"Do not touch me. Do not dare touch me."

He looked to her with darkened eyes. "Ye cannot possibly think that is true." Darach searched her face. "I came to explain and make ye see why I went there."

The clenching of her jaw made her back teeth protest, but she could not keep from it. Isobel forced her gaze up and met his. "It is the truth. I do not begrudge ye what ye feel. However, I do not forgive the insult to me and our marriage. For this affront in front of everyone will not be soon forgotten. How could ye?"

"I needed to know…"

"It matters not to me what yer reasons are. I cannot bear to hear any reasoning ye might have. What is done is over now and cannot be repaired."

When he looked about the room, taking in that all her belongings had been moved, he turned back to her. "Ye cannot remain here. Yer place is with me, in our bedchamber."

When he went to continue, Isobel held up her hand. "As yer wife, I cannot deny ye access to my body. I am fully aware of it. However, I will not lie next to ye every night while knowing ye love another. Ye cannot force me to do it."

"Isobel," he began, and she interrupted.

"Darach. I will not bend on this."

"Fine," he replied through clenched teeth and left the room.

It was as if the room became completely devoid of everything when he walked out. The very air seeming to still; her lungs expanding as she fought to draw it in. Her marriage was now what it was supposed to be from the very beginning. An arrangement. A contract between two clans for an alliance. That she was part of it, was only to ensure the agreement was sealed.

It was foolish to think otherwise. To hope for a love match or at least a marriage where her husband would be loyal.

Isobel vowed not to cry. She would not allow herself the pain of any more physical torture than she'd already experienced. At the sound of gulls calling, Isobel went to the window and stared out for a long time.

WHEN LAST MEAL came, she managed to keep a calm façade when entering the great hall. Conversations lulled, the room's atmosphere changing as those present attempted to look to her without it seeming obvious.

How exactly was one to act upon first seeing the lady of the keep right after her husband proved his love for another? With pity or concern? Or perhaps, like most there, with curiosity to see the interaction between them.

Darach stood upon her approach and held out her chair. When she lowered to sit, he did as well and turned to her. "Ye look very pretty this evening."

Knowing everyone watched, Isobel forced a smile. "Ye look very different to me today."

For a moment, a crease formed between his brow, but then he only nodded.

People kept turning to look at them and then murmuring to one another. Isobel wanted to stand up and run from the room. Either that or do something that would give even more fodder for gossip. She envisioned pouring ale over Darach's head or tossing his plate onto his lap.

"Would ye like some fruit?" Darach asked, his gaze locked on her.

"No, I would not," Isobel replied shortly. A servant approached, and with her gaze lowered poured ale into her cup. The young woman's hand shook as she met Isobel's gaze.

"Is something wrong, Ila?" Darach asked the servant, who started at the question.

"Nay, my laird, all is well," the girl slid at look to Isobel, waiting to be dismissed.

"Ye may go," Isobel said, and the girl scurried off. "I imagine, she murmured, "it will be a while before they stop feeling pity for me."

Darach tracked the servant girl's progress, then looked to the people sitting around the tables. Instantly everyone avoided eye contact, looking to one another or their food. It seemed her husband finally noticed what he'd been oblivious to. No one would look directly at him or Isobel.

"This is ridiculous," he said under his breath and looked to

Stuart, who sat on his right. They spoke to one another in soft tones, so Isobel could not hear.

She turned to her left where Lady Mariel sat eating in silence. She looked about to cry.

"Do not fret for me," Isobel told her and patted her hand.

"I never wished this for ye," she replied, her eyes shiny with unshed tears. After taking a long drink from her cup, Lady Mariel met her gaze. "I am here for ye, Isobel. Be assured in this, I am with ye."

After the meal, it was customary for the family to go into a parlor and spend time together before going to bed. Just the thought of being around the Ross men made her physically ill. Needing to be away and alone, she ignored Darach's attempt to take her elbow and instead walked toward the stairs.

Beatrice caught up with her. "Would ye like me to come sit with ye for a bit?" Her sister began to head in the direction of Isobel's bedchamber, but she stopped her.

"No, let us go to yer room instead."

"Of course."

Isobel was glad that her sister did not try to touch her or coddle her in any way, because at that moment, it would have been too hard to control her emotions.

They walked into Beatrice's room and sat on the bed. Beatrice searched her face. "Dear sister, I hate to leave ye now," her sister admitted. "I think I should remain here a bit longer."

"Do what ye wish. Whether ye are here or not, this situation will resolve itself. I do not wish ye to remain because of me. I am sure Mother and Father miss ye terribly."

"Will ye not miss me then?" Beatrice smiled at her.

"If ye decided to remain here to live, I would be very happy. Of course, ye would have to ask for Father and Mother's permission."

Beatrice pouted. "I doubt they will give it. Mother has decided I am to be married. She'll need me close by to shove in front of suitors."

"Ye make it sound so very pleasurable," Isobel teased. "Let us send a messenger asking for permission. We can request that ye spend the winter here."

"What will ye do? It is as if the entire clan knows what happened," Beatrice sighed. "It is all so horrible... what Darach did."

She'd been asking herself the same question over and over. "I will continue as normal. Help manage the household, help the poor and elderly. I will take my walks and sketch. On occasion, I imagine having to lay with him. But other than that, I do not face a horrible life."

Beatrice covered her hand. "Ye are so very brave. I am not sure I could be so."

"I have a different opinion sister," Isobel said. "Ye are far stronger than I am. For in the face of scrutiny and not being chosen by the laird, ye continued forth, doing what ye could to work for the betterment of his clan. Never have ye waivered in any way, despite yer fear of the beastly Ross men."

Her sister's laughter was like bells to Isobel's ears. She couldn't help but smile and sense that in truth, she would be fine. The current experience would make her a stronger woman and a better lady of the keep.

That her marriage was not a love match was not something unexpected, what was unacceptable was to allow any kind of emotional involvement.

"I best go to bed. Sleep well, sister." Isobel pressed a kiss to Beatrice's brow. "Do not write to our parents without me. We shall do it together."

Her sister nodded. "Very well. Sleep well."

Upon entering her bedchamber, she found a new sketch-book on her bed. The book was beautiful, the paper of the best quality. Instantly her mood lifted a bit as she leafed through the book, touching each page and considering what different scenes she'd draw on each one.

It had to be Beatrice who'd purchased it. She'd hug her sister and thank her in the morning.

When she went to the dressing table, atop it was a beautiful wooden box that was tied closed with a green velvet ribbon.

Slowly she untied the ribbon and let out a breath at seeing a beautiful art set of pencils and chalks in an array of colors.

Never had she seen anything so beautiful. Had the peddler carried this? Strange that such items would be on a peddler's wagon.

The gift was not from Beatrice but from Darach. Intuitively, she knew it. There were other things in the room. She found a necklace in a black velvet bag on the table next to the bed, as well as a buttery soft set of gloves. Across the bed was a soft linen robe with lace on the cuffs.

The elaborate gifts didn't touch her in the way they would have when he must have ordered them from the peddler. These kinds of things could never take the place of his love or faithfulness. Instead, they were a stark reminder of the absence of such things.

She placed everything on the bed atop the dressing gown and wrapped them.

When Annis came, she handed her the bundle. "Please get rid of these. Perhaps put them in the laird's study."

While Annis was gone, she undressed and loosed her hair. There was a knock on the door and Isobel let out a long breath.

She opened it to find Lady Mariel. When she motioned for the woman to enter, she shook her head. "I only came to wish ye rest and tell ye that tomorrow we will take our first meal in my sitting room as has been my custom and perhaps now it can become yers as well."

"Thank ye," Isobel said.

Lady Mariel passed her son in the corridor without speaking to him. Darach looked tired. She was sure with all that happened, he needed to seek his bed.

"Sleep well Isobel," he said meeting her gaze.

Without response, she closed the door and leaned on it. "I will not cry," she murmured.

CHAPTER NINETEEN

W HEN BEATRICE WALKED into the family parlor and found it empty, she wanted to squeal with joy. It was by far her favorite room in the entire keep. Large windows allowed one to look out to the sea just past rocky hillsides. In the distance, sheep grazed without care under a blue sky with a cloud here and there, seeming to be placed just right by an artist.

A table and pair of chairs by the window gave her the perfect place to sit and pen a letter to her parents. Already two nights had passed since her sister's humiliation and a sense of heaviness remained thick in the home.

What she'd tell her parents eluded her, so she waited for inspiration on how to start the letter. As much as she appreciated, Isobel's offer to help her write it, her sister was not in the right frame of mind to do so at the moment. This was her project to complete, and it had to be carefully written.

She curled into one of the chairs, tucking her feet under her, and sighed happily. It was the perfect place to think. She tapped her chin with a finger while looking out the window considering how to plead her case.

Her family could not know what happened, that her sister had been humiliated by the laird. Not that it would be anything that would affect things. Afterall, they'd married her off without care if it was a love match or not. However, her mother would be upset at hearing that Isobel was dejected.

Smiling, she sighed. Perhaps she could convince her mother of being courted. It could mean Lady Macdonald would travel there immediately just to ensure the courtship was with someone they approved of and to ensure she didn't do anything inappropriate. She was after all quite impulsive at times.

"Who should I choose?" Beatrice said out loud.

At hearing a door open, she peered around the chair but didn't see anyone. Deciding the person must have been looking for someone, she went back to peering out the window.

A few moments later, distinct footsteps made it known someone had entered.

Beatrice peered around the chair again. It was Duncan. The massive man had entered making little noise.

Despite being tall, with bulging muscles all over, he moved with an assured fluid grace.

"Miss Beatrice," he said by way of greeting.

"Mister Duncan," Beatrice replied, a shiver traveling through her. "I can leave if ye require privacy."

He shook his head and looked down the blank parchment and quill. "I came searching for ye actually. I am going to North Uist the day after tomorrow and can escort ye back home."

"I am about to write a letter to my parents. My sister needs me here, so I plan to remain for a while longer. I cannot bear leaving her right now."

Instead of a reply, he kept his gaze averted, peering out the window to the scenery. "I can deliver that letter then."

"Thank ye. I will write it now."

He finally met her gaze, and she could not keep her eyes from widening. Like his brothers Stuart, Ewan, and Gideon, he had dark brown hair and the same face structure. However, his eyes were not like the others. One was the familiar hazel, while the other a dark brown.

Keeping his eyes downcast, he turned away. "Tomorrow is fine. I will not leave until after last meal."

She reached for his forearm to stop him from walking away. "Yer eyes," she began. "They are quite unique. My eldest brother, Evander, has eyes like yers, two different colors. One is blue, like mine, the other is brown."

It was as if he didn't believe her and searched her face waiting for what else she would say.

"Ye must meet him when ye go to deliver my letter. He does not like the feature and complains about it. Although I have to admit, women seem to find it quite attractive."

Duncan frowned, which told her that he didn't agree with the statement. "If he is there, I will meet him."

"Good," Beatrice replied, and when she looked back up, he was already walking out. "A man of few words."

It was strange that she'd felt at ease with Duncan Ross. While speaking to him, she'd felt as if he would be protective of her. Unlike most men who considered her no more than a spoiled doll, he'd not looked down at her with disdain or forced patience.

Beatrice blew out a breath and lifted her quill. What could she say to convince her mother, who would then talk her father into allowing her to remain at Keep Ross longer?

Her family had plans for her to marry soon, so it would take a very good reason for them to allow her to remain longer. However, her mother was keen on her marrying a Ross.

Her lips curved. She would tell her mother that one of the Ross men was courting her. It was possible her mother would return, but it would not be right away.

But who?

One by one, she considered the single brothers. "Stuart seemed brokenhearted over the breaking of his betrothal. Gideon was too much like her, brash and without care. Caelan was distant and in her opinion a bit aloof. She considered Duncan last. He was older and if she were to be honest, the most handsome. It was hard to picture him in a romantic way. Not that he was off-putting at all and beneath the hard-muscled façade, she sensed vulnerability.

He would be a good choice, being he did not live there in the keep, it would be easier to keep her mother from accidentally running into him alone. The fact he would be delivering the letter would help it seem true.

Excited to remain there longer and provide comfort to her sister, she began writing.

HIS MOTHER WALKED into the study and Darach pushed the ledger away.

To his astonishment, his mother went to the sideboard and poured whisky into a glass and drank from it.

"Whatever were ye thinking son?"

Of course, he instantly knew what she spoke of. "Mother, I need yer counsel. What can I do to make things right?" Darach followed suit and also went to the sideboard to pour a whiskey.

"I do not think ye can do anything at this time to change things. The damage is done. Ye have publicly proclaimed to hold yer mistress in higher regard than yer wife."

The words were like lashes to his bare skin. He'd made a horrible mistake and now he paid the price. Isobel paid a higher one. Humiliation and pity followed her.

They sat in silence for a few moments. Darach standing by the sideboard and his mother in a chair. She motioned to her empty glass and he refilled it and handed it to her. This time she took only a sip.

Her gaze pinned him. "I am not sure what can be done at this point Darach. What do ye expect me to tell ye? That all will be well? That yer marriage is not beyond repair? If ye would not have allowed yer passions to direct ye, then perhaps yer wife would not be humiliated as such."

"I went to find out about the bairn. Lilia is not and has not been my lover since before Isobel came here. I made a mistake going there. I am very aware now. I am not used to thinking about a wife first."

When his mother looked at him with disappointment, Darach wished to be back at Uisdein's keep, not knowing his fate. It had been a dark moment when he'd considered that he might not live. That he considered he might not leave a descendent was not unnatural. And yet, in truth, he could have waited to find out."

"Mother, I beg of yet to intercede for me with Isobel. Help me make this right, or at least as much as possible."

She gave him a sad smile. "Son, ye are a young laird. Yer

father never gave ye neither advice nor example of how to be a good leader. I am proud of ye, for the way ye look after the people."

He waited for what she'd say next, hoping for enlightenment.

When she sighed, his hopes were dashed. "The only advice I can offer is that ye give her time. Do not press her to forgive ye. Remain near at all times and do yer best to remain pleasant to her. It may be difficult as she will not make it easy for ye."

The room seemed to close in on him after she walked out. The silence made the humming in his ears sound louder. He wanted to race up the stairs and find out Isobel's reaction to his gifts. However, if he were in her place, the gifts would probably make things worse at this time.

When Annis, Isobel's companion rapped at the door and stood there with a bundle, his thoughts were confirmed.

"My laird, Lady Isobel requested that I bring this here," she said with a hint of disdain in her voice. "Where should I put them?"

He motioned to the table where he and his council sat around to hold weekly meetings. "On the table."

With measured steps, she placed the bundle down with care and walked back out.

He drank the rest of the whisky and slammed the glass on the sideboard just as Duncan entered.

His brother looked at the glass that his mother had left. "Drinking with a ghost?"

"Mother was just here."

"If she drank, she must be very cross with ye," Duncan said lifting the same glass and pouring more amber liquid into it. "What does she advise?"

"That I give Isobel time and be patient." Darach raked fingers through his hair. "I should have thought this through. There are so many other things I should be doing, but my mind cannot rest knowing I've hurt my wife so publicly."

"Do ye think she will be forgiving?" Duncan asked, sitting. "Ye must know her enough to discern."

"I have not been married to her long enough to be able to assume anything about my wife. She is kind, but this has wounded her deeply."

"All ye can do is wait and do as Mother says." Duncan changed the subject. "Darach, I am returning to my home after last meal tomorrow. I will spend a day there to prepare for travel and hope to head to North Uist by mid-day the day after."

On his desk, two letters were already written. "Come and fetch the missives before leaving. One is for the Macdonald, the other is for the ship captain that ye are meeting. Ensure he is aware we are to be the only investors in his shipment and should be informed immediately upon his return."

"I will," Duncan replied. "One more thing. Yer wife's sister does not wish to leave. She is sending a letter to her parents requesting to remain longer. Wants to be here for yer wife."

"I am not surprised."

"I am sure this will resolve itself over time. For now, be on yer best behavior, brother."

Trudging up the stairs, Darach did not look forward to sleeping in his empty bed again. However, it was too soon to ask for Isobel's company.

When arriving at his door, he looked to his wife's and took a step toward it. And then another.

CHAPTER TWENTY

I SOBEL TOSSED AND turned, unable to sleep. Her mind raced over the events of the last few days. So much had changed between her and Darach, while at the same time everything else remained the same.

There were tasks to see to. After all, the keep would not run itself, and Lady Mariel had begun the process of handing more responsibilities to her. Starting the next day, she would no longer hide in her room.

She had nothing to be ashamed of.

If her husband was unfaithful and disloyal, it was he who should be embarrassed by his actions and lack of propriety.

It didn't matter that her heart was broken, or that sadness filled her. One day it would become normalcy. There was only one way to continue. With dignity and bravery. If Lady Mariel had shown her anything, it was to turn one's focus elsewhere. To pursuits that gave satisfaction and joy.

She considered the beautiful art items that Darach had purchased. She would have to ask the peddler to purchase duplicates. It would be too much of a reminder of what he did, to use the ones he'd bought.

Turning to her other side, Isobel closed her eyes and tried to calm her thoughts, but immediately, she pictured Darach across the corridor. Sleeping in the large bed they once shared.

How long before he shared it with another woman?

The door opened with a soft creak. Isobel didn't bother to look. If Annis or Beatrice came to check on her, she would pretend to sleep. They would then leave satisfied she was well.

Moments later, Darach came to view as he rounded the bed. Isobel made sure to keep her eyelids lifted just enough to watch him through her lashes.

He paced in front of the fireplace as if trying to decide what to do. Then he sat in a chair and began removing his boots. After that, he removed his breeches, remaining only in a tunic.

With measured moves, he neared the bed and lifted the bedding.

The warmth of his nearness almost made her move away, but she persisted in pretending to sleep.

Darach laid on his back and stared at the ceiling. Then ever so slowly, he picked up her left hand, held it against his chest, and promptly fell asleep.

If she were to snatch her hand away it would wake him, so instead, she lay still as his breathing evened out. Under her palm, the steady beating of his heart and heat soothed her. Despite herself, Isobel inhaled his familiar scent, realizing she'd missed him terribly.

With a herculean effort, she held back tears that threatened and forced sleep to come.

THE DOOR CLOSING woke Isobel, she lifted her head to look and confirmed Darach had slipped out. Sighing she fell back onto the bed. She would have to inform him, he was not welcome to sneak into her bedchamber. Why bother with her own room if he was to intrude at will?

Admittedly, upon his coming to her bed, she'd fallen into the first deep sleep since the last time they'd shared a bed. However, she was not about to allow sentimentality to sully her convictions.

Annis entered moments later with a cup and saucer in hand. Behind her, a maid walked in with a pitcher of warm water for Isobel's morning ablutions. It had been necessary when sharing a bed with Darach as they'd made love so often. Now, however, the additional washing was not as necessary.

Nonetheless, she did not say anything and went about preparing for the day.

"How would ye like yer hair today Lady Isobel?" Annis asked pulling her hair up and meeting her gaze in the mirror.

"Whichever way yer please. Something simple is fine."

Once she dressed, again in a serviceable dress, as she planned to spend time reviewing the gardens, she lifted her shawl and opened the door.

Darach stood beside the door to his bedchamber. He leaned on the wall but straightened upon her appearance. Something in her stomach fluttered at seeing him.

"May I walk ye to first meal?"

"Yer mother has invited me to break my fast in her sitting room in the mornings."

"It is customary for ye to eat with me," he replied in a soft tone. "But if ye wish to eat with my mother, I will go with ye there instead."

Isobel was at a loss. "Yer mother is expecting me."

Taking her elbow, he guided her to the end of the corridor and then to the right where his mother's quarters were. When they walked in, the table was set with four plates and cups, as Beatrice and Ella often ate there as well. If Lady Mariel was surprised at her son's appearance, she did not act like it. Instead, she stood and went to him.

"Son, I am so glad that ye join us today," she said lifting her face to accept his kiss to the cheek.

Darach guided Isobel to a chair and lowered to another next to her. A servant hurriedly placed a plate and cup before him. "We only have tea, Laird," the girl explained. "I can go fetch ale."

"Tea is fine," he replied and lifted Isobel's plate. Once he served her something of each item, a slice of cold meat, cheese, and bread. He left off buttering the bread knowing she did not care for it.

Beatrice met Isobel's gaze with questions and Isobel gave a light shrug and a droll look.

"What will be done about the Uisdein?" Ella asked. Obviously the only one not ill at ease at Darach's presence.

"I declared clan Uisdein our enemy. Therefore, we will not trade with them, nor will his people be allowed past our borders."

"What of families?" Beatrice asked, unable to remain quiet. "Are there not families that are joined by marriage who belong to both clans?"

He nodded. "Aye. And they will have to choose a side."

Lady Mariel changed the conversation to the normal talk of the daily duties, as Darach ate and listened in silence. Every so often he added suggestions, which surprised Isobel to the amount of knowledge he had when it came to running the household.

"All of my sons helped me when lads," Lady Mariel informed her and Beatrice. "Ye see, their father would not have any duties for them until they reached ten and three, before then, he preferred I keep them out of the way. Therefore, they did household duties. In my opinion, it prepared them better for life on their own, if it came to be."

The more she learned about Lady Mariel, the more Isobel admired her and understood why her sons were so loyal to her. She was the single reliant and constant presence in their lives.

"When I am blessed with bairns, I hope to be like ye, Lady Mariel," Isobel said and then covered her mouth with one hand at realizing the implications of her statement.

If Darach found her words surprising, he didn't act so. Unfortunately, Beatrice was as enthusiastic as ever.

"There is no doubt in my mind that ye will be the best mother," she said looking around the table. "Isobel has been the best sister, always caring for me and looking after my safety and such. She will be a wonderful mother."

"Laird," a guard said, standing at the door. "There is a messenger here for ye."

"Duty calls," he said pushing back from the table. He stood and walked out speaking to the guard, immediately back to being Laird Ross.

Everyone looked to her at his absence.

"Did ye forgive him already?" Beatrice asked, her arms crossed. "So soon?"

"I have not come to the place where I can," Isobel explained. "He was standing in the corridor waiting for me and insisted on accompanying me." She left out the part of him coming to her bed the night before as Isobel wasn't sure what to make of it.

Lady Mariel lifted her cup to her lips and sipped. "He has a lot of making up to do. I suggest ye do not forgive him until yer good and ready. What my son did was utterly thoughtless."

"But ye must admit Mother, it was so unlike him," Ella said coming to her brother's defense. "Darach has always been fair. Although at times too stern, he does care about what others feel."

Beatrice bristled. "He insulted my sister greatly."

"I do not argue it," Ella replied. "However, please do not think less of him. He made a mistake. A horrible mistake." She sniffed and wiped away a tear. "Please do not hate my brother, Isobel. Do not make yer marriage like Mother's."

Isobel rushed around the table to hug Ella. "I do not hate him. He is my husband. It will take me time to forgive his unfaithfulness and learn to live with the fact he may keep a lover."

"He will not keep a lover," Lady Mariel insisted. "He asked that I find a husband for her. Lilia admitted to Darach that the bairn is not his but would not name the father. I believe my son when he tells me he has not lain with her since before yer arrival Isobel."

Beatrice spoke up for Isobel as she could not think of what to say. "I hope my sister will come to trust him because like ye, Ella, I wish for them a happy marriage. A love match."

THERE WAS A lot of work to be done in the gardens. Large cabbages, leeks, and beetroot flourished along with carrots that were ready to be harvested. A waist-high wall had been built around the area to keep livestock out which had a beautifully crafted iron gate. On the far corner of the garden area was a shed that held gardening tools, baskets, and lines of herbs hung to dry. Just outside the shed, there was a small table and a bench for resting. It was one of Isobel's favorite places and she planned to sit there and sketch the garden before it was harvested.

Thankfully, they would be able to stretch out the offerings through the winter. Once all the harvesting was done, it would be time to allow the soil to rest.

Isobel looked on as weeds were plucked and the items needed for that day's last meal were gathered. "Give me the basket," she said to a maid, and accepted a basket filled with vegetables to take inside.

When she turned, Darach stood by the gate. His gaze moved from her face to the basket and he extended a hand. "I will take it inside. Wait here for me."

The women working in the garden stopped and gawked when Isobel turned to look at them. She released the basket handle and pulled her shawl tighter around her shoulders while waiting for him to return.

It would have been interesting to see Greer's face when the laird brought in the basket of food for preparing.

He reappeared with Albie on his heels. "Would ye like to walk with us?"

Knowing the women looked on, she nodded. "Of course."

Taking her elbow, Darach guided her across the courtyard and through the front gates. As per usual, the dog shot off toward the forest, while they continued walking.

"The messenger is from Laird MacNeil. An invitation for

me to come there to discuss clan relations."

Her stomach clenched at the thought he'd be leaving once again and perhaps another incident like the one before would occur.

"When do ye plan to leave?"

"I am not sure. There are things I must see to first. A dispute between two prominent landowners. There was a report that Cairn may be heading toward North Uist."

Isobel remained silent. As much as she hoped to not feel betrayed, she could not get past it. If only there was a way to know for sure that he did not have feelings for Lilia still.

"Isobel," Darach said and waited for her to look up. "Remember the first fortnight after our marriage? That we were to remain near to each other for all those days?"

"Of course."

"I wish to do it again. Not force ye to more than my presence. I wish to convey my loyalty but am at a loss other than to say again and again that I regret my actions and wish there was a way to undo them."

"It cannot be undone."

Darach let out a long breath. "I did not have relations with her. Nor do I care for her in the way I do for ye. Because honesty is important, I will admit to caring for her well-being, as she was my companion—of sorts—for a long time."

"Ye and I are husband and wife," Isobel began. "We will remain so. Whatever else may be, that is not to change."

"I wish for more than just a marriage. I wish for a relationship with ye."

Albie reappeared, dragging a large branch, and Isobel had to smile at the dog's antics. Darach ran to meet his dog and

231

broke off a smaller branch throwing it for Albie to run after. They walked and took turns throwing the branch for a bit as Darach told her about the Ross clan's history when it came to the MacNeil's.

It seemed they were allies based on Lady Mariel's marriage to the late laird. However, through Darach's father's inability to keep to his promises and dealings with mutual enemies, like the Uisdein, relations were now strained.

It was an enjoyable afternoon, although, as soon as they returned, Isobel rushed inside, needing time away from him, and the pain being near him caused.

She paced in the parlor, unable to keep still.

Lady Mariel entered a few moments later and upon seeing her, sat down with a book, giving Isobel time to settle.

"Tell me what to do," Isobel said, lowering to a chair. "I feel so very conflicted."

Her mother-in-law's face softened. "Take yer time. Trust yer heart and ask God that he allow ye to forgive yer husband."

ISOBEL WOKE FROM a deep slumber to soft snores and realized Darach was asleep next to her. He'd obviously had to work late because of all his duties he'd pushed aside to spend time with her.

Unable to move because he held her hand to his chest again, she listened to his breathing.

She finally gave up the idea of moving away from him and snuggled closer as sleep lulled her back.

Like the day before and the one before that, he was gone

from the bed when she woke, but upon opening the door, he waited for her outside in the hallway.

"Darach, ye have many duties to attend to. I cannot allow ye to spend so much time coddling me."

Instead of a reply, he placed his hand at the small of her back. "Are we going to the great hall or Mother's sitting room?"

"The great hall," she said, knowing that it was time the people who came early to speak to Darach see them together.

Surprisingly, most of those there did not take much notice of them as they went to the high board and sat. Darach served her before taking his own plate, seeming to be content to remain in silent companionship with her.

Deciding it would be interesting to hear the people's issues and grievances, Isobel remained next to Darach as he and Stuart dealt with those that came forward. It was surprising how many people were still there by late morning.

It was exhausting to watch and listen to as Darach spoke with the people to work out their differences. If things became complicated, then he would seek counsel from either Stuart or another council member and dole out decisions.

He took his time with each situation, never belittling the people, even those with petty grievances, and in her opinion, gave fair decisions.

Murmuring began from the back of the room.

Darach stiffened as Lilia walked in through the main entrance. She was not alone; beside her was a man who looked to be a bit older, and Isobel wondered if perhaps the man was Lilia's relative.

Did he come to demand her child's father marry her?

Darach motioned for Lilia and the man to come forward, ahead of others who waited. No one seemed to mind, curiosity taking precedence over it being their turn.

The woman weaved her arm through the man's as they made their way forward. The way she held her head up was admirable as she neared and lowered to a curtsy before Darach. Upon straightening, her pride-filled gaze lifted.

"Laird," the man began. "I am Tavish Robertson, from the eastern shore of yer lands. I have a good home and plenty of livestock. Lilia has agreed to my proposal of marriage. I can provide a good life for her if ye would permit us to marry."

Isobel felt her eyes widen.

Darach studied the pair. "I know ye. My brother Duncan and I went to yer father when younger, to learn to be better at manning birlinns."

"Aye, ye did," the man said with a soft smile.

"Lilia, are ye willing to marry Tavish Robertson and be a good wife to him?" Darach asked the question never looking away from Lilia.

The woman's eyes became bright with unshed tears. "I would very much like to be married and raise a family with Mr. Robertson."

"Very well," Darach said. "Ye have my permission to marry. Ye are a good man Tavish Robertson, I trust ye will treat Lilia well."

Lilia slid a look to Isobel with what she would describe as curiosity.

As propriety dictated, Lilia and Robertson were invited to stay for last meal, but they declined. They were to travel immediately back to his homeland to get married.

By the time Darach announced hearings for the day were over, he looked exhausted. He turned to her. "I have to meet with the council to decide about the MacNeil and also about patrols for the borders and lands. Do ye wish to come with me?"

Isobel shook her head. "Nay. I must see about the staff's duties and ensure all is well with preparations for last meal." Before standing, she reached for Darach's hand and pressed hers over it. "Ye are a good and fair leader."

Their gazes met for a long moment and Isobel saw truth in his eyes. He was not lying about what had transpired. He had not been disloyal to her. What she had to forgive was the insult of him going to someone else before her. And who was she to hold anger in her heart for so long.

Darach was holding himself accountable and doing all in his power to prove his remorse.

When Isobel walked away, she hurried to find Annis.

"Is something wrong Lady Isobel?" Annis asked jumping to her feet when Isobel burst through the door of the servant's hall.

"I need yer help," Isobel said. "I am moving my belongings back to the bedchamber I first shared with my husband."

Annis smiled widely. "Thank God. I was not sure how long I was to pretend he did not sleep in yer bed."

Isobel shook her head unable to keep from smiling at Annis.

CHAPTER TWENTY-ONE

S TUART, EWAN, AND Gideon sat around the table in
Darach's study. Across from him, two elders, who'd been
members of the council, also remained.

"We've sent warriors after Cairn. They will find him. It is
doubtful he will remain hidden for long," Ewan said and
shook his head. "What did he truly hope to accomplish by
plotting against us?"

Fury evident in his expression, Gideon pounded his fist on
the table. "It matters not what he hoped for. What he will
receive is hanging for it. We cannot allow his kind of treachery
to go unpunished."

Darach agreed. "Once he returns and we question him, he
will be put to death. Duncan is seeing to arresting several
others who the farmer identified as being at the meeting and
asking to lead a rebellion. They too will be punished."

The late laird had often executed people for things that in
his opinion, merited a more lenient punishment. Now he
wondered if by doing the same, he'd been seen as another
tyrant and people would fear him. He did not wish to rule by
fear, but by gaining people's loyalty.

"I think only the leader should be executed," Stuart said in
a solemn tone. "He may have misled them. People were
hungry, their families with little hope. It was easy for Cairn to

place the blame on ye, lying to them that ye would be like our father."

"They should have known better," Gideon argued. "Ignorance is not an excuse."

"I disagree," Ewan said. "It was too soon. Darach hadn't the opportunity yet to prove himself. It is only recently that they are beginning to see he leads in a fairer manner."

Darach looked to the elders. "What is yer opinion?"

The oldest council member, Amis Ross, a distant cousin, scratched his beard. "Treachery is a very serious offense. Leaders in a rebellion against a laird, should all be punished. I believe that Cairn misled the people and only looked to gain power for himself." He paused to meet Darach's gaze.

"Yer father was an unfair and cruel man. The clan expected ye to be no different. They have little options, so the men who followed the treacherous Cairn hoped for the betterment of their families."

Stuart huffed but remained silent.

Amis continued, "I advise that those who planned to be leaders in this be whipped and jailed for a minimum of six months."

Darach nodded. "Thank ye, Amis. I plan to speak to Duncan and discuss both this situation, as well as him coming here to stay when I am away at the MacNeil's. Mother and Isobel are accompanying me. Keep our home safe in my absence."

"Catriona is near to giving birth, I will not be here as much as I would like," Ewan said with a wide grin.

The men all congratulated his brother.

"I am happy for ye brother and cannot wait to meet my niece or nephew." Darach said.

"Catriona insists it will be a boy," Ewan said, still grinning.

AFTER THE COUNCIL members left, only Stuart remained to help him review the assignments for guardsmen, a letter of invitation to the MacLeod, and several other items that had to be seen to before he left.

It was late before he walked out of his study because he'd taken time away from his duties to spend part of the day with Isobel.

And yet, he had no regrets because the more time they spent together, the stronger he felt for his wife. She was not only beautiful, but extremely caring, kind, and intelligent.

His mother had insisted she would agree to travel to Barra with them and he hoped it was true.

Perhaps getting away from the keep would help her warm to him more.

Never had he missed a woman so much as he did Isobel. Although he knew it was his right to take her body, he would wait for her to be willing. Forcing himself upon her would only make things worse and no matter how much he ached for her, he was not willing to make a second mistake.

The corridor loomed long as he headed to the bedchambers. He stopped in front of Isobel's door and then turned to the one they'd shared. Still undecided, he reached for the door handle to Isobel's chamber.

Upon entering, he couldn't see anything. The room was pitch black, with no fire in the hearth. He lit a candle that was on the table next to the door, giving him enough light to see.

The room was bare, empty of his wife and her items.

Panic squeezed at his chest. Had Isobel left without him

knowing? No, it was impossible. The guards would have surely stopped her and informed him.

Just then Ramey turned the corner toward him. "Good night, Laird. Do ye wish assistance?"

"No, go seek yer bed."

When the man turned away, Darach called his name. "Do ye know where my wife is?"

The valet gave him a strange look. "I cannot say for certain, Laird. Have ye looked in yer bedchamber?"

"Sleep well," Darach said, dismissing him. The last thing he needed was a witness upon learning his wife had left or moved farther away to keep him from joining her at night.

When he opened the door to his bedchamber, he immediately looked to the bed. On his bed was Isobel sleeping soundly.

He then gathered the courage to look around the room. Her comb and ribbons were on the dressing table, her robe over the trunk at the end of the bed. He walked to the wardrobe on the far side and opened it to find all her gowns had been returned.

Unsure of what to do since for the last several nights, his routine had been disrupted, he sat down for a moment.

"Darach?"

Isobel was sitting up looking at him. "Are ye coming to bed?"

"Aye." Overcome with emotion, he couldn't formulate any other words in that moment.

The light from the fire reflected about the room, casting a wavy pattern across the space. Isobel looked like a siren, her hair loose about her shoulders, and nightdress untied at the throat so that the tops of her breasts were revealed.

"I cannot keep from ye," Darach admitted. "I desire to make love to ye until the sun rises."

Her tongue darted out, licking first her top lip and then the bottom. "I ached for ye, Darach, so very much."

Needing no further encouragement, he ripped the clothing from his body, tossing it wherever it fell, uncaring of anything other than to go to the beauty in his bed.

Their mouths met in an urgent kiss of passion and need, while he helped her pull the nightdress off.

The feel of her soft body against his was almost enough to send him to release, but he held back, needing time to relish what he'd been missing for so long. Isobel against him, under him, writhing and calling his name.

"Take me, I cannot wait," Isobel urged. "I am on fire."

"As am I," Darach said slipping his hand between her legs to stroke her sex. She would come fast the first time, he needed her to find a fast release so that they could climb her second crest together.

When her nails dug into his shoulders, he knew she was close. Darach lowered, trailing his tongue down the center of her body until reaching her apex. Then he took her sex into his mouth and lapped at the engorged nub with the tip of his tongue.

Isobel lifted up from the bed with cries of passion that were like music to his ears. "Oh Darach!" she called out, her entire body shivering. He blew on her sex and suckled at the center causing her to shudder in a hard release.

As she settled, he kissed her thighs, her hips, and her stomach, allowing her time to catch her breath. When he sought her mouth, his restraint gave way and he pushed inside her.

The sensation was like no other, he gasped and blew out

short breaths to keep from releasing then and there.

He drove in deeper before moving out and thrusting back into her beautiful body.

"Yes," Isobel urged as he continued driving in and out of her, sinking deeper and deeper, unable to keep from losing control.

The release was long and so overwhelming, he cried out, Darach's entire body tensing with uncontrollable shudders. Isobel writhed under him, lost as well, in her own cresting.

When Darach collapsed over her, he was drenched in sweat, their bodies slick with the result of lovemaking and he loved it.

She bit his shoulder playfully. "That was agreeable."

"Aye, I found it pleasant," he teased back.

They both chuckled, but quieted when he took her mouth. He meant to keep to his word to make love to her until the sun rose.

"I AM HAPPY that ye are going with yer husband to Barra to visit the MacNeil," Beatrice said, watching as Isobel packed. "It will be just myself and Ella here."

Isobel smiled at her sister. "Lady Mariel is going as well; she is a MacNeil like our mother and has family there."

Beatrice nodded. "When Mother and I visit in the spring, we will go to Barra to visit as well. Perhaps, ye and Lady Mariel will go with us."

"I think it sounds like a wonderful idea," Isobel said, meaning it. "I still cannot believe our parents allowed ye to remain. Whatever did ye put in that letter?"

With a secretive expression, Beatrice stood and then smiled. "Ye look happy sister."

"I am content for now. Happiness does not feel far away."

Just then the door opened and Darach entered.

"I was just leaving," Beatrice said and, after a saucy wink, walked out.

Isobel accepted a kiss to the temple from Darach. "I cannot go for a walk just yet. I have much to do. Perhaps one of yer brothers can take Albie out today."

"I agree and will do as ye say. I also have much to see to today." He pressed his lips to hers. "That is not what I came in here for."

"Oh." Isobel looked up at him reveling in his arms and the warmth of his gaze. "Why then?"

"I forgot to tell ye something."

Whatever he was about to say made her a bit anxious. "What is it, Darach?"

"Ye should know, wife, that I have fallen deeply in love with ye. I cannot imagine a life without ye beside me."

Her heart soared, and tears stung her eyes.

Immediately Darach hugged her to him. "Are ye upset?"

Pushing back, she chuckled. "No, I am happy. These are happy tears." Isobel let out a sigh and gazed up at her handsome husband. "I believe that I fell in love with ye on the day we married. It was inevitable, I suppose. Ye being so handsome and roguish."

His lips curved, and he pressed his forehead to hers. "I am glad that ours has become a love match."

Happier than any other time in her life, Isobel pressed her head to his chest and listened to the familiar thuds of his heart. A heart that belonged only to her.

The Clan Ross of the Hebrides saga continues with Duncan's story.
The Beast

How can a such a hauntingly beautiful man hold so much ugliness within?

Duncan Ross' inner scars are even more horrifying that the visible ones. Unable to control his rages, he hides himself away from his close-knit family. He has long accepted the painful truth that he will never have a family or a wife. When a beautiful woman tells her family they are courting, he is forced to make an agonizing decision that will break her heart and shatter his lonely soul.

As the pampered daughter of a powerful laird, Beatrice Macdonald is rarely taken seriously. When her sister marries Laird Ross, she fights to remain at Keep Ross to ensure her sister is treated well. In order to make her case, Beatrice lies and tells her that Duncan Ross is courting her for marriage. However, the more she gets to know the reclusive man and his secrets, the more she realizes that she picked the wrong Ross brother for the ruse.

The Beast

ABOUT THE AUTHOR

Enticing. Engaging. Romance.

USA Today Bestselling Author Hildie McQueen writes strong brooding alphas who meet their match in feisty brave heroines. If you like stories with a mixture of passion, drama and humor, you will love Hildie's storytelling where love wins every single time!

A fan of all things pink, Paris, and four legged creatures, Hildie resides in eastern Georgia, USA, with her super-hero husband Kurt and three little yappy dogs.

Join my reader group on Facebook: bit.ly/31YCee1
Sign up for my newsletter and get a free book! goo.gl/jLzPTA
Visit her website at www.hildiemcqueen.com
Facebook: facebook.com/HildieMcQueen
Twitter: twitter.com/authorhildie
Instagram instagram.com/hildiemcqueenwriter